Henry Arthur Jones

The Masqueraders

Henry Arthur Jones

The Masqueraders

ISBN/EAN: 9783337396978

Printed in Europe, USA, Canada, Australia, Japan

Cover: Foto ©Andreas Hilbeck / pixelio.de

More available books at **www.hansebooks.com**

yet possessed of the wish to try my luck again, and, I trust, under
more favorable auspices. However, the bit of scenery which I
mentioned in the first part of this letter has remained a bright spot
in a dark setting. Perhaps you know its location and caught it
with your camera. With the mosquitoes brushed away, it was the
pleasantest ground we struck in our foolish expedition to find a
jumping-off place in the North Pole direction. Trusting you may
be able to comply with this (I hope not impertinent) request, I
remain, etc.''

This is an experience, indeed an especially amusing one, and
rather out of the ordinary. The story of "cussed" fishing luck is
exactly in line with what has been stated in the beginning of this
chapter, and one that but few fishermen would so candidly relate.
However, I can add that the writer did carry out his "wish to try
my luck again," and the trip proved to be so thoroughly satisfactory, that he has often repeated the trial since.

Before concluding the chapter, and the work as well, some
space properly should be devoted to—(the defence of, I was about
to write in error)—the rarely excelled fighting powers of the
ouananiche. Through the medium of occasional articles appearing
in publications on fishing, a few letters received, and a very few
complaints that I have heard personally, I find that an extremely
small percentage of seekers after the Lake St. John fish raise the
cry that its gameness is greatly overrated. I have referred to this
subject several times in preceding chapters, but a final word cannot
prove to be amiss.

I fear that these unbelievers must be classed as a variety of
the "doubting Thomas" family, since they raise their voice or pen
in opposition to the consensus of opinion as expressed by the most
noted anglers in the country. All have hooked and brought to
net, and at varying times during the season, ouananiche that were
logy and faint-hearted. Such also has been the experience of those
fortunate anglers who have met and conquered the salmon, bass
and trout. They do not condemn them, however, for their inac-
tivity at that particular time, since they know that history has
credited them with battling powers which they are honestly entitled
to. These same noted fishermen have made the history of the

ouananiche as well, and the facts set forth would require more than the present very small minority vote to change them.

Any number of quotations from well-known fishing authorities could be given, but this is not at all necessary, since, as is well known, they all agree perfectly in regard to the fighting and lasting powers of the "little salmon." It is to be admitted that one cannot, as an enthusiast, write on a favorite subject without the recollection of past sport, and the imagination as well adding a little high coloring. Nature at times presents most gorgeous sunset hues and tints, colors, which if we were to describe or reproduce, would be classed as highly exaggerated. Why not, therefore, if Nature's occasional high colorings are natural and true, should not the occasional high-colored claims for the ouananiche be equally so?

In conclusion, I wish to state that the experiences given, the stories of the varying sport had, and the numbers of fish taken in catches mentioned, are not in the least out of the ordinary in any particular. The large number of sportsmen who have made not one alone, but a number of visits to and about Lake St. John, will almost universally give witness to this effect. Moreover, the fact must not be overlooked that the same possibilities for sport and success in fishing are still extant as in the past, and that thousands of square miles of virgin wilderness yet await the sportsman discoverer. Be governed by the when, where and how as set forth herein ; then eliminate the attempt to accomplish all in a few days, or the inability to meet occasional disappointment, and but one result can follow—satisfaction and success heretofore unknown. You will feel amply repaid by seeing the wonderful beauties of the trip alone, but add to this the satisfaction of perfect sport secured, and you will return believing that the most satisfactory location for sportsmen to visit at the present day is Lake St. John and its surrounding wilderness.

THE

MASQUERADERS

A PLAY IN FOUR ACTS

BY

HENRY ARTHUR JONES

AUTHOR OF

'THE TEMPTER,' 'THE CRUSADERS,' 'THE DANCING GIRL,' 'JUDAH,'
'THE MIDDLEMAN,' 'THE LIARS,' 'THE CASE OF REBELLIOUS
SUSAN,' 'THE TRIUMPH OF THE PHILISTINES,'. 'MICHAEL
AND HIS LOST ANGEL,' 'THE ROGUE'S COMEDY,'
'THE PHYSICIAN,' 'THE GOAL,' 'SAINTS AND
SINNERS,' 'THE MANŒUVRES
OF JANE,' ETC.

London

MACMILLAN AND CO., Limited

NEW YORK : THE MACMILLAN COMPANY

1899

Produced by Mr. George Alexander at the St. James's Theatre on 28th April 1894.

PERSONS REPRESENTED

DAVID REMON.

SIR BRICE SKENE.

MONTAGU LUSHINGTON.

EDDIE REMON.

THE EARL OF CRANDOVER, Master of the Crandover Hunt.

HON. PERCY BLANCHFLOWER.

SIR WINCHMORE WILLS, M.D.

GEORGE COPELAND.

FANCOURT.

CARTER.

RANDALL.

RODNEY.

SHARLAND.

JIMMY STOKES, an old huntsman.

BRINKLER, proprietor of " The Stag."

THOMSON.

DULCIE LARONDIE.

HELEN LARONDIE, her sister.

CHARLEY WISHANGER, afterwards Lady Shalford.

LADY CLARICE REINDEAN, Lord Crandover's daughter.

LADY CRANDOVER.

Guests, Dancers, Fox-hunters, Hotel Servants, and Waiters.

ACT I

SCENE—THE COURTYARD OF THE STAG HOTEL AND
ASSEMBLY ROOMS AT CRANDOVER.

(*Three years and a half pass.*)

ACT II

SCENE—DRAWING-ROOM AT LADY SKENE'S.

(*Nine months pass.*)

ACT III

SCENE—PRIVATE SITTING-ROOM AT THE HÔTEL PRINCE
DE GALLES, NICE.

ACT IV

SCENE—THE OBSERVATORY ON MONT GARIDELLI,
MARITIME ALPS, NEAR NICE.

The following is a copy of the original play-bill of · "The Masqueraders."

ST. JAMES'S THEATRE.

Sole Lessee and Manager—MR. GEORGE ALEXANDER.

To-night, Saturday, 28th April 1894, and every
evening at eight o'clock,

A new and original modern Play, in Four Acts,

By HENRY ARTHUR JONES,

ENTITLED

THE MASQUERADERS

DAVID REMON . . .	Mr. George Alexander.
SIR BRICE SKENE . . .	Mr. Herbert Waring.
MONTAGU LUSHINGTON . .	Mr. Elliott.
EDDIE REMON	Mr. H. V. Esmond.
LORD CRANDOVER (Master of the Crandover Hunt) . . .	Mr. Ian Robertson.
HON. PERCY BLANCHFLOWER .	Mr. A. Vane-Tempest.
SIR WINCHMORE WILLS, M.D. .	Mr. Graeme Goring.
GEORGE COPELAND . . .	Mr. Ben Webster.
FANCOURT . . .	Mr. Arthur Royston.
CARTER . . .	Mr. Guy Lane-Coulson.
RANDALL . .	Mr. J. A. Bentham.
RODNEY . . .	Mr. F. Kinsey Peile.
SHARLAND	Mr. A. Bromley-Davenport.
JIMMY STOKES (an old whip) .	Mr. William H. Day.
BRINKLER (proprietor of "The Stag")	Mr. Alfred Holles.
THOMSON . . .	Mr. F. Loftus.
A Servant . . .	Mr. Theo Stewart.

DULCIE LARONDIE . . . Mrs. Patrick Campbell.
HELEN LARONDIE (her sister) . Miss Granville.
CHARLEY WISHANGER (afterwards
  Lady Shalford) . . . . Miss Irene Vanbrugh.
LADY CLARICE REINDEAN (Lord
  Crandover's daughter) . . Miss Beryl Faber.
LADY CRANDOVER . . . Mrs. Edward Saker.

Guests, Dancers, Fox-hunters, Hotel Servants, and Waiters.

THE PRESENT DAY.

ACT I.

SCENE—THE STAG HOTEL AND ASSEMBLY ROOMS
AT CRANDOVER.

(*Four years pass.*)

ACT II.

SCENE—DRAWING-ROOM AT LADY SKENE'S.

(*Nine months pass.*)

ACT III.

SCENE—PRIVATE SITTING-ROOM AT THE HÔTEL
PRINCE DE GALLES, NICE.

ACT IV.

SCENE—THE OBSERVATORY ON MONT GARIDELLI,
MARITIME ALPS, NEAR NICE.

ACT I

SCENE—THE OLD COURTYARD OF THE STAG HOTEL
AND ASSEMBLY ROOMS AT CRANDOVER, ROOFED
IN TO FORM A HALL.

*Along right is a bar-counter, surmounted by a glass case-
ment and windows, which open and shut down on to
the counter. In the middle of the counter is a lid,
which lifts up and forms doorway. At the back are
steps leading to the Crandover Assembly Rooms.
On the left the large old-fashioned gateway of the
Inn. Running all round are the old galleries re-
maining from coaching times. Plants and banners
hung about the hall. On the outside of bar is hung
a subscription list, in which the words " Widow and
Orphans " and "Dick Ramsden " are discernible.
Dancing in the rooms beyond. Amongst the company
are* LORD CRANDOVER, LADY CRANDOVER, LADY
CLARICE REINDEAN, CHARLEY WISHANGER. *The
dance concludes, the couples disengage themselves,
some of them come from the Assembly Rooms into
the Hall.* BRINKLER, *the proprietor of the Stag*

ℍ   B

Hotel, is crossing the stage.·, MONTAGU LUSHINGTON, *a modern young man, is coming downstairs.*

LORD CRANDOVER (*a jovial English aristocrat of about fifty, speaks to* BRINKLER). Devilish rum start this of Miss Larondie's, Brinkler.

BRIN. (*with a grin*). Yes, my lord.

LORD CRAN. Where is she?

BRIN. (*pointing off into the bar*, L.). In the bar there.
(*They all look off, and show great interest.*
MONTAGU LUSHINGTON *joins the group.*)

CHAR. (*a very fast, mannish little woman, to* MONTAGU). Not bad, eh?

MON. Exquisite. That divine poise of the arm as she draws the handle of the beer machine is really quite priceless.

LORD CRAN. Does she bring you much business, Brinkler?

BRIN. Well, she's brought me two good customers, my lord.

LORD CRAN. Who are they?

BRIN. One of them is Sir Brice Skene, my lord.
(LADY CRANDOVER *exchanges a look with* LADY CLARICE.)

LADY CRAN. Is Sir Brice often here?
(LADY CLARICE *is showing interest.*)

BRIN. He's almost lived here lately, my lady.

LADY CLAR. (*to* LADY CRANDOVER, *aside, bitterly*). What did I tell you?

LORD CRAN.　Who's the other customer?

BRIN.　That mad gentleman that lives at Gerard's Heath, Mr. Remon.　There he is in the bar now.

(*They all look off, and show great interest.*)

MON.　That pale individual who is dallying with claret in the corner?

BRIN.　Yes; that's sixty-eight Mouton Rothschild. I get it specially for him.　Fancy drinking Mouton Rothschild!

CHAR.　The man's looking at us.

SIR BRICE *enters from back, comes down gradually to group.*

LORD CRAN.　He's an astronomer, isn't he?

BRIN.　I believe he is something in that line, my lord.　And he's got a little brother who is likewise touched.

MON.　With the stars, or the·barmaid?

BRIN.　Miss Larondie isn't exactly a barmaid, is she, my lord?

LORD CRAN.　No; her mother was distantly related to the Skenes.　Her father came of a good old French family.

LADY CRAN.　The girl might have done well for herself.　We used to receive her family at the Court, and when her father died I interested myself to get her a situation as a governess in a Christian family. But she behaved very badly.

Mon. When one is a governess in a Christian family, one is compelled to behave badly for the sake of the higher morality.

Lady Cran. Miss Larondie has thoroughly lost caste. And I should take it as a great favour if Mr. Brinkler would see that she has no chance of—of misconducting herself with——

(Sir Brice *has come up, and* Lady Crandover *stops embarrassed when she sees him.*)

Sir Brice. With whom? Is Miss Larondie about to misconduct herself, Brinkler?

Brin. No, Sir Brice, I trust not.

Sir Brice (*to* Lady Crandover). Have you any reason for supposing that Miss Larondie is about to misconduct herself, Lady Crandover?

Lady Cran. (*embarrassed*). I—I am surprised, Sir Brice——

Sir Brice. Have you any reason for supposing that Miss Larondie is about to misconduct herself?

Lady Cran. No.

Sir Brice (*politely*). Thank you.

(*Goes off into the bar. In crossing the bar he has to pass* Lady Clarice, *he bows to her with extreme politeness, she bites her lips, and returns his bow. Exit* Sir Brice *into bar.*)

Lady Clar. (*to her mother, aside*). Oh, I can't bear it!

Lady Cran. Hush!

LADY CLAR. He has gone to that girl.

(*The next dance begins. The stage gradually clears.*)

CHAR. Our dance, Monty.

MON. (*giving arm*). So your vestal self is dedicate to matrimony and Sir Digby Shalford ?

CHAR. Yes ; he's a trifle washed out ; but we are frightfully hard up, and you didn't ask me.

MON. My dear Charley, marriage is the last insult one offers to a woman whom one respects. Love if you please——

CHAR. Thanks. We'll think about it. By the way, you'll stand a chance with Clarice now Sir Brice has cut her. Her connections would be useful to you.

MON. What would Crandover settle on her ?

CHAR. Not much. Clarice would tell me. I'll ask her. What would you do it for? A thousand a year ?

MON. (*reproachfully*). My dear Charley, don't hurt my self-respect. (*They go into the ball-room.*)

Enter EDDIE REMON, *a delicate boy of about twenty, highly refined, overstrung, unbalanced. He is followed by* GEORGE COPELAND, *a bearded, athletic man about forty.*

COP. But what's he doing here ?

EDDIE. Sun-gazing.

COP. Sun-gazing?

EDDIE. Yes. Look ! Here's his sun. She's

dragging him through space, and where the devil they're going to, I don't know.

Enter DULCIE LARONDIE *from bar.   She stands for a moment looking off.*   EDDIE *and* COPELAND *stand aside up stage.*

DUL. (*speaking off into the outer bar.   She has a large key in her hand*).   I've forgotten the candle. Sir Brice, would you mind bringing me that candle?

DAVID REMON *enters from bar, with the lighted candle in his hand.   He is a man of about forty, pale, studious, philosophic-looking.*   SIR BRICE *follows quickly, and the two men stand facing each other.*

SIR BRICE.   Give me that candle.

DAVID.   Miss Larondie——(*Appealing to* DULCIE.)

DUL. (*stands coquettishly looking at both of them*). That one shall light me to the cellar who makes himself the most ridiculous over it.

DAVID (*coming towards her*).   That will be myself.

SIR BRICE.   Give me that candle.

DUL.   Sir Brice, Mr. Remon will make himself far more ridiculous than you.

SIR BRICE.   Then let him light you.

(*Exit into bar.   REMON is carrying the candle towards the cellar door perfectly straight in his hands.   DULCIE turns to him.*)

DUL.   You're carrying that candle on one side; you're dropping the grease. (*He looks at her, holds it much on one side, and drops the grease.*) That's better. (*She unlocks the cellar door, stands a moment or two looking him up and down with comic inspection.*) Yes, I think that will do. You look very well. Would you mind waiting here till I come back?

> (*Gravely blows out the candle, enters the cellar, and shuts the door after her.* DAVID *stands there. Pause.* COPELAND *comes behind him, claps him on the shoulder.*)

COP. Davy!

DAVID (*turns round, cordially*). My dear fellow! (*Very warm hand-shaking.*) You're coming to stay?

> (EDDIE *creeps off to the bar and watches there.*)

COP. No, to say good-bye. I catch the night mail back, and to-morrow I'm off to Alaska. I'm sick of this nineteenth-century civilisation. I must do a bit of climbing, and get myself re-oxidised.

DAVID. What is it this time?

COP. Mount Saint Elias, 19,000 feet high, and snow at the sea-level.

EDDIE. Davy, your bottle of claret is here in the bar.

DAVID (*looking at the cellar door*). But Miss Larondie has not come back from the cellar.

EDDIE. She went up the other stairs. She's in the bar talking to Sir Brice Skene. (DAVID *goes to the bar, looks off, shows intense mortification. The band strikes up a very bright dance-tune.* EDDIE *puts his fingers in his ears.*) Oh! oh! oh! Those wretched musicians!

Cop. What's the matter?

EDDIE. They are playing horribly in tune, as if the world were full of harmony. I must get a tin kettle and put them out.

> (DAVID *goes up to the bar, shows intense mortification, conquers it. Exit* EDDIE *into bar.*)

BRINKLER *enters with a bottle and glasses.*

DAVID. Brinkler, my claret here.

> (BRINKLER *brings bottle in cradle and two glasses, puts them down on the other side of stage.*)

BRIN. Mouton Rothschild, sixty-eight.

DAVID. So I'm mad to drink the finest vintages, eh Brinkler? (BRINKLER *looks surprised.*) I heard you say so.

BRIN. Well, it is unusual, sir.

DAVID. You're right. A man must be mad who drinks the rarest wines when he can get salted beer and doctored gin. Still, you must humour me, Brinkler. (BRINKLER *seems puzzled and stands apart.*) Though what's the good of climbing Mount Elias, I don't know. (*Turning to* COPELAND.)

Cop. To get to the top of it.

DAVID. But what's the good of getting to the top of it?

Cop. What's the good of getting to the top of anything? You've spent the last dozen years of your life and nearly blinded yourself to solve the mystery of sun-spots.

DAVID.   But sun-spots are practical.

COP.   Practical ?

DAVID.   Who solves the mystery of sun-spots may show the way to control the future harvests of the world ; and who controls the harvests of the world will provide cheaper swipes and smaller beer for Brinkler's grandchildren, eh Brinkler ?

BRIN. (*comes forward*).   Sir ?

DAVID.   I was saying that the elect of the earth, and by the elect of the earth I mean every man who has a vote, may get cheaper swipes when I have solved my problem of sun-spots.

BRIN.   Sir ?

DAVID. Your grandchildren shall be amply provided for, Brinkler.   (*Turns to* COPELAND.)   Drink. (*Exit* BRINKLER *puzzled.*)   A prosperous voyage and a safe return, old fellow.   (*Drinks.*)   I've drunk to your folly, now drink to mine.

COP.   Tell me all about it, Davy.   It is folly, then ?

DAVID.   No, if folly is happiness, folly is the greatest wisdom.

COP.   You are happy, then ?

DAVID (*nods*).   Yes.   And wretched, beyond all telling.

COP.   Why ?

DAVID.   I shall never win her.   She'll never be mine, George.   And if she were,—that might be the saddest thing of all.

COP.   How ?

DAVID. When the desired one becomes the possessed one, her beauty fades. I love her, George, and I want to keep on loving her. (COPELAND *laughs*.) Laugh at me! I laugh at myself. I was forty-two last August. You know pretty much what my life has been. Drink one glass, old boy, to the days when we were twenty-five, and to our old loves.

COP. (*drinks*). Our old loves. Your last one, Davy?

DAVID. Ah! She soured me, but she didn't break my heart. And she drove me to my sun-spots. So God bless her! God bless them all! Whatever I've been in practice, George, in theory I've always had the most perfect loyalty to womankind of any man that ever breathed. (COPELAND *laughs*.) Don't laugh, you rascal! I mean it! I've always kept my reverence for them, and I've always known that some day or the other I should meet one who would make me worship her with the purest devotion a man can feel for a woman.

COP. And you have met her?

DAVID (*nods, looking towards bar*). She's in there, flirting with the choicest blackguard in England.

COP. You poor dear fool! You always would pay half-a-crown for anything you could get for twopence.

DAVID. Yes, but I always knew what a fool I was. Do you think I don't know what a fool I am now? George, it's not any empress, not any goddess, but just that girl in the bar there that owns me body and soul.

COP. Pack up your traps and come to Alaska and forget her.

DAVID (*hand on his heart*). She's packed herself here, and here she'll lie snug and warm till all grows cold. (*Looking over to bar.*) And that blackguard is talking to her !

COP. Who is he ?

DAVID. Sir Brice Skene.

COP. The racing man ?

DAVID. Yes. He's rich. George, if he——

COP. If he—what ?

DAVID. He shook hands with her last night. When his finger-tips touched hers, I felt I could kill him, George. And if he—if he—No, I wrong her ! She's a good woman. And yet, damn him, he has twenty thousand a year——

COP. Is it a question of money ?

DAVID. What do you mean ?

COP. I've not a single near relation in the world. My father left me, I suppose, from two to three hundred thousand pounds. (*Holds out hand.*) Davy, say the word——

DAVID. No, George.

COP. Why should you hesitate ?

DAVID. I don't want it. I've just enough for my wants. I've only Eddie to provide for. And I've only one extravagance. (*Tapping the bottle.*) I love good wine, and plenty—not too much—of it.

Cop. But if you were rich—perhaps she——

David. Thanks, George; I won't buy her.

Cop. You're welcome.

David. I know it.

Cop. By Jove, I've only just time to catch the mail. Good-bye, Davy. (*They stand hand in hand for some moments.*) I've left a couple of thousands at Coutts' in your name.

David. I shan't use it.

Cop. As you please.

David. How long shall you be away?

Cop. I shan't come back till I've stood on Mount Saint Elias. Can I do anything for you?

David. Yes. Tell me the quality of the moonshine on the top.

Cop. The same quality as your moonshine here, and just as real.

David. Is anything real? (*Looking at the fox-hunters and dancers.*) I've lived so long alone with only Eddie that the world has grown quite spectral to me. Look at these phantoms! (*Pointing to the fox-hunters and dancers.*) Is anything real, George?

Cop. Yes; that two thousand at Coutts'.

David. And friendship. Friendship is real, isn't it? (*Shaking hands.*) God bless you, George. I'll come to the station with you.

(*As he is going off* Dulcie *enters from bar,* Sir Brice Skene *following her.*)

DAVID (*sees her*). No! (*Shakes hands.*) Don't break your neck over Mount Saint Elias!

COP. Don't break your heart over a woman!

DAVID. Yes, I shall. After all I'm only playing at life, and so I'll break my heart over her—in play.

COP. Stick to your sun-spots! (*Exit.*)

SIR BRICE (*catching sight of the subscription list*). What a confounded lot of widows and orphans there are in the world!

DAVID (*sitting on the other side*). Miss Larondie is an orphan.

DUL. Yes, or I shouldn't be here. I wonder why all we superfluous women were sent into the world!

SIR BRICE (*leaning over the bar*). You are not superfluous. You are indispensable.

DUL. To whom?

SIR BRICE. To me.

DUL. (*makes a profound mock courtesy*). You do me proud. (*Calls to* DAVID.) Mr. Remon, can you tell me why I was sent into the world?

DAVID. To be indispensable to Sir Brice Skene.

SIR BRICE (*aside to* DULCIE). Why do you talk to that fellow?

DUL. (*aside to* SIR BRICE). Oh, he amuses me. I can make such a fool of him, and—I'm so sick of this.

SIR BRICE. I'll send you my new mare on Friday. Come to the meet.

DUL. I daren't. What would everybody say?

SIR BRICE. What does it matter? I'll send you the mare.

DUL. No. They'd all cut me. Would your sister chaperon me? You know she wouldn't.

SIR BRICE. My dear—you've made an awful mistake.

DUL. Don't call me your dear. I won't have it.

SIR BRICE (*with a little laugh*). My dear, you've made an awful mistake, and there's only one way out of it.

DUL. I don't wish to get out of it. Let them laugh at me, and cut me. I can bear it.

SIR BRICE. Don't be a fool. If I were to offer you——(*in a low voice*).

DUL. (*stops him*). No. Pray don't. I shan't take it.

SIR BRICE (*bending nearer to her.* DAVID *has risen and come near to them*). But if I were to offer you——

DAVID (*to* SIR BRICE). Will you give me those matches, please?

SIR BRICE (*leaning away from the bar*). Take them.

(DAVID *takes them, walks back to table, seats himself at it.* SIR BRICE *follows, seats himself at the other side of the table.*)

Enter JIMMY STOKES, *an old huntsman in an old hunting suit.*

DUL.   Oh, Jimmy Jimmy Stokes, I'm so glad to see you!   How are you, Jimmy Jimmy Stokes?

JIMMY (*beaming old fellow of about seventy*).   Oh, I'm just tol-lol, miss, for a hold 'un.   How's yourself, miss?

DUL.   Oh, this isn't myself, Jimmy.   Myself's dead and buried, and when I come back to life I shall find this queer creature has been playing all sorts of mad pranks in my absence.   Sit down, Jimmy Jimmy Stokes, and put a name on it.

JIMMY.   Well, just a little wee drop of gin, miss, if I ain't intruding.

DUL.   Intruding, Jimmy?   You ought to be welcome at any meet of the Crandover.

JIMMY.   Head whip five-and-thirty years, I was. And thinks I, I'll look in to-night.   So I washes myself up, putts on my old whip's coat, and here I be as bold as brass.   You see, miss, I be a privileged party, I be.   Thank you, miss—Woa, woa, miss—woa!

(SIR BRICE *and* DAVID *have been sitting at table, looking at each other.*)

SIR BRICE.   You spoke?

DAVID.   No.   (*The look is continued for some moments.*)

SIR BRICE (*folds his arms over the table, leans over them to* DAVID).   What the devil do you mean?

DAVID (*folds his arms over the table so that they meet* SIR BRICE'S, *leans over them so that the two men's faces almost touch).* I mean to kill you if you dishonour her.

SIR BRICE. You'll kill me?

DAVID. I'll kill you.

SIR BRICE. I'll have her one way or the other.

DAVID. You're warned.

> (SIR BRICE *rises, goes towards* DULCIE, *is about to speak to her.* DAVID *turns round and looks at him.* SIR BRICE *stops, calls out to* DULCIE, *who is talking over the bar to* JIMMY STOKES.)

SIR BRICE. Miss Larondie, I'll send you the mare on Friday. (*Exit into ball-room.* DULCIE *shakes her head,* SIR BRICE *looks at* DAVID *and exit.*)

JIMMY. Well, here's luck to you, miss, and I wish I could see you going across the country with the C. H. as you used—that's all the harm I wish you, for you was a sweet, pretty figure on horseback, you was, and you rode straight, you and your father, wire and all—you rode straight.

DUL. Don't remind me of old times, Jimmy. (*Turns to* DAVID *mischievously.*) Mr. Remon, it's getting late. Isn't it time you were going?

DAVID. (*rises*). Good-night.

DUL. Good-night. (*As he is passing out to door she calls out to him again.*) Mr. Remon——

DAVID (*stops*).

DUL. I've something to say to you.

DAVID (*coming to her*). What is it?

DUL. (*tapping her forehead impatiently*). It's gone! Would you mind waiting there till I think what it is?

DAVID. Certainly.

DUL. That's so good of you. (*Looks him up and down a little while mischievously.*) Can I give you a book while you wait? Here's "Bradshaw," the "Turf Guide," this week's "Sporting Times."

DAVID. I shouldn't understand it. I'll look at you.

DUL. Do you understand me?

DAVID. Perfectly.

DUL. I don't understand you.

DAVID. You will some day.

> (*The dance has finished, and a crowd of young men dancers, FANCOURT, CARTER, RANDALL, RODNEY, SHARLAND, and others, come chattering and laughing to the bar, and shout for drinks together.*)

FAN. I say, Miss Larondie, I'm dying for a whisky and soda.

CAR. Lemon squash.

RAN. A baby bottle of jump.

ROD. Brandy and soda.

FAN. Don't serve him, Miss Larondie. He's three parts squiffy already.

ROD. Shut up, Fan.

SHAR. A gin cocktail, Miss Larondie, and I'll show you how to mix it.

FAN. Don't trust him, miss. He wants to sneak a sample of your spirits for the public analyst.

Rod.   Serve me first, Miss Larondie, and I'll give you a guinea for Dick Ramsden's widow.

(*General hubbub and clatter.*)

Dul.   Order, order, gentlemen! Jimmy Stokes, take this gentleman's guinea and go round with this list, and see what you can get for poor Dick's family.

(Jimmy *takes the subscription list, and is seen to go round with it to several of the bystanders, and talk to them in dumb show.*)

Fan.   I'll come behind and help you, miss.

(*Lifts up the lid of the counter, and tries to push in.*)

Rod. (*pushing him back*).   Sling, you animal! I'm going to be under-barmaid here.

(*They both push in behind the bar.*)

Fan.   No, you don't. Now, gents, your orders, and no larking with us poor unprotected females.

(*Putting his arm round* Dulcie's *waist.*)

Helen Larondie *enters and stands watching* Dulcie.

Dul. (*indignantly to* Fancourt).   How dare you?

Rod. (*on the other side, puts his arm round her waist.—to* Fancourt).   How dare you?

Dul. (*disengaging herself indignantly*).   Pass out! Do you hear? Pass out! (*Showing them the way out. Sees* Helen *standing there, shows great shame.*) Nell!

Fan. (*seizes* Rodney *by the collar and runs him out*).   Pass out! Do you hear? Pass out!

(*Runs him out of the bar.*)

BRINKLER *enters.*

BRIN. Gentlemen! Gentlemen! If you please! gentlemen! If you please!

DUL. Mr. Brinkler, my sister has come for me. Would you mind waiting on these gentlemen?

(*They clamour round* BRINKLER, *repeating their orders for drinks.* DULCIE *goes to her sister.*)

DUL. Nell!   (*Kisses her.*)

HELEN. My dear.

DUL. Come and talk to me. (*Takes her up to where* DAVID *is standing. She catches sight of* DAVID, *who, has been watching the scene with a mixture of bitterness and amusement. Seeing* DAVID.) Mr. Remon—I had forgotten you.

DAVID. You had such pleasant companions.

DUL. I have wasted your time.

DAVID. It's of no value.

DUL. But I'm afraid I've made you rather foolish.

DAVID. In a world of fools it's a distinction to play the fool for you. In a world of shadows, what does it matter what part one plays? Good-night.

DUL. No, come again.

DAVID. It's closing time.

DUL. But we shall be late to-night. Come again by and by.

DAVID. By and by.   (*Exit.*)

HELEN. Who is that?

DUL. His name's Remon. He has haunted the

place for the last month. He's in love with me. I can make him do any foolish thing I please. (BRINKLER *serves the young men with drinks. The music strikes up again, and they gradually go off, leaving the stage with only* DULCIE *and* HELEN *on it.*) Nell, I'm so glad—what makes you come so late?

HELEN (*a soft-voiced, gentle woman of about thirty, in a nurse's dress*). I've just had a telegram to go and nurse a typhoid case at Moorbrow, so I shan't see you for a few weeks. You still like it here?

DUL. (*rather defiantly*). Yes. It's livelier than being a governess, and it isn't so horrid as nursing typhoid.

HELEN (*smiling*). Dear, there's nothing horrid about nursing. It's just like a mother and her baby.

DUL. How awfully sweet *that* must be. (*Looking at her sister.*) How patiently you take our come-down, Nell. Instead of rebelling and hating everybody as I do, you've just gone and nursed all these dirty people and made yourself quite happy over it.

HELEN. I've found out the secret of living.

DUL. What's that?

HELEN. Forget yourself. Deny yourself. Renounce yourself. It's out of the fashion just now. But some day the world will hear that message again.

DUL. (*looking at* HELEN *with admiration*). I wish I was good like you, Nell. No, I don't. I don't want to deny myself, or renounce myself, or forget myself. I want to enjoy myself, and to see life.

That's why I screwed up my courage and answered Brinkler's advertisement, and came here.

HELEN. And are you enjoying yourself?

DUL. (*defiantly*). Yes, after a fashion. I wish I was a man, or one of those girls upstairs. Why should they have all the pleasure and happiness of life?

HELEN. You're sure they have all the pleasure and happiness of life?

DUL. At any rate they've got what I want. Oh, how I long for life! How I could enjoy it! Hark! (*Dance music swells.*) Isn't that dance maddening? I must dance! (*Begins.*) Oh, Nell, I was made for society! Oh, for London! for pleasure! To be somebody in the world! How I would worship any man who would raise me to a position! And wouldn't I repay him! What parties I'd give! I'd have all London at my feet! I could do it! I know I could! Oh, is there anybody who will take me out of this dead-alive hole and give me the life I was made for?

(*Flings herself wildly round, half dancing, and drops her head into* HELEN'S *lap sobbing.*)

HELEN (*stroking* DULCIE'S *hair, very softly*). My poor Dulcie! I knew you weren't happy here.

DUL. I hate it! I hate it! Nell, don't be surprised if I do something desperate before long.

HELEN. Dulcie, you'll do nothing wrong.

(*Lifting up* DULCIE'S *head, looking keenly at her.*)

DUL. What do you mean? Nell, you know I wouldn't. Kiss me, ducky. Say you know I wouldn't.

HELEN (*kisses her*). I don't think you would, but —when I came in and saw those two men——

DUL. (*quickly*). Boys. They meant nothing. One has to put up with a good deal here. Men aren't nice creatures.

HELEN. Dulcie, you must come away from this.

DUL. Where? What can I do? I wish somebody would marry me. What wouldn't I give to cut Lady Clarice as she cut me to-night !

HELEN. Did she cut you ?

DUL. Yes. She gave me one look—Nell, if she looks at me again like that, I don't care what happens, I shall box her ears.

HELEN. Dulcie !

DUL. But if she cuts me, Sir Brice has cut her. And he pays me no end of attention.

HELEN. You're not growing friendly with Sir Brice ?

DUL. No—yes—he's always paying me compliments, and asking me to take presents.

HELEN. You haven't taken his presents ?

DUL. No. Don't fear, Nell, I'll take nothing from him except—if he were really fond of me, I'd marry him, Nell.

HELEN. No, dear, no. He's not a good man.

DUL. Nell, there aren't any good men left in the world. The race is extinct. I daresay Sir Brice is as good as the rest, and if he were to ask me I should say "yes." (HELEN *shakes her head.*) Yes, I should, Nell. And I should make him a good wife, Nell, for there are the makings of a good wife in me. I should say "yes," and oh, wouldn't I like to see Lady Clarice's face when she hears the news.

HELEN. I hope he won't ask you, Dulcie.

DUL. Stranger things have happened.

HELEN. I must be going. I've to watch a fever case to-night.

DUL. (*twining* HELEN'S *arms round her neck*). I wish I could have a fever.

HELEN. Dulcie!

DUL. It would be so lovely to be nursed by you. (*Hugging her.*) I shall never love a man as I love you, Nell. But I suppose that's a different kind of love. (HELEN *sighs.*) What makes you sigh?

HELEN. Good-bye, Dulcie.

DUL. Good-bye, you dear, nice, soft, warm, comforting thing. You're as good as a boa, or a muff, or a poultice to me. I'll let you out this way. It's nearer for you.

(*Exeunt* HELEN *and* DULCIE *through bar.*)

SIR BRICE *enters from ball-room, followed by* LADY CRANDOVER, LADY CLARICE *following.* LADY CLARICE *goes and sits down quite apart.*

LADY CRAN. Sir Brice!

SIR BRICE (*turns, stops*).

LADY CRAN. (*somewhat embarrassed*).   Do you know what people are saying of you?

SIR BRICE.   I haven't an idea.   But whatever it is, don't stop them.   (*Going.*)

LADY CRAN. (*stops him*).   Sir Brice.   All through the season you have paid the most marked attention to Clarice.

SIR BRICE.   I admire Lady Clarice immensely. I have a very ingenuous nature, and perhaps I allowed it to become too apparent.

LADY CRAN.   You allowed it to become so apparent that every one in the county supposed as an honourable man——

SIR BRICE.   Ah, that's a nice point, isn't it?   If Crandover thinks I have behaved dishonourably, the Englishman's three remedies are open to him—he can write a letter to the "Times," or he can bring an action, or—he can horsewhip me.   Personally, I'm indifferent which course he takes.   Excuse me.

(*Goes off into the bar.*)

LADY CRAN. (*enraged, and almost in tears, goes to* CLARICE).   My dear, he's a brute!   What an awful life his wife will have!

LADY CLAR.   Then why did you run after him? Why did you let me encourage him?

LADY CRAN.   Clarice, he has twenty thousand a year.

LADY CLAR.   But everybody says he'll run through it in a few years.   He lost fifty thousand on the Leger alone.

LADY CRAN.   I know.   Oh yes, he'll soon get /
through it.   Well, now you've lost him, it's a great
comfort to think what a perfect brute he is.   You've
had a lucky escape.

DULCIE *re-enters from bar.*   JIMMY *re-enters with sub-*
scription list, and a crowd of young fellows following
him.

LADY CLAR. (*watching* DULCIE).   Yes, but I don't
like being thrown aside for that miss there.

Enter from ball-room MONTY, CHARLEY WISHANGER,
and other dancers gradually.

DUL.   What luck, Jimmy?
JIMMY (*shakes his head*).
DUL. (*takes the subscription list from him*).   Oh,
Jimmy Jimmy Stokes, when we keep a Punch and
Judy show, I'll never send you round with the hat.
JIMMY.   Ah, miss, we know how you could get a
peck of money for 'em—don't we, Mr. Fancourt?
FAN.   By Jove, yes.   Jimmy has made a splendid
suggestion, Miss Larondie.   The only question is,
will you agree to it?
DUL.   What is it, Jimmy?
JIMMY.   You back me up, miss, that's all, will you?
DUL.   Certainly.   Anything to keep Mrs. Ramsden
and her chickabiddies out of the workhouse.   I

always feel, you know, Jimmy, that it was through me that Dick was killed.

FAN.   Through you, Miss Larondie?

DUL.   I was leading across Drubhill.   I took the drop into the road.   Dick was next behind.   His horse stumbled and (*shudders*) they picked him up dead.

(*All the young fellows have crowded round and listen.*)

JIMMY.   'Twas me as picked him up if you remember, miss, and took him home, I did, ah, it's three years ago last February, yes, and I broke the news to his wife, I did, and what's more, I helped to lay Dick out, I did, and I says to his wife, "Don't take on now, you foolish woman," I says, "why," I says, "it might have been *felo-de-se*."   But it were a nasty drop jump, miss, a nasty drop jump.

DUL.   And if I hadn't taken it, perhaps Dick might have been alive now.

JIMMY.   Not he, not he.   Dick'd have drunk himself to death before this.   He was a royal soul, Dick was.   And if you'll only back me up, we'll raise a little fortune for Mrs. Ramsden in no time.

DUL.   Very well, Jimmy.   But what is this plan, eh, Mr. Fancourt?

FAN.   Tell her, Jimmy.   You started it.

JIMMY.   Well, miss, seeing all these young gents here, it struck me as, human nature being what it is, and no getting over it, no offence I hope to anybody, but if you was to offer to sell one, mind you, only one, of your kisses to the highest bidder——

DUL. (*indignantly*). What?

MON. A very excellent and original suggestion!

DUL. The idea! What nonsense!

FAN. Nonsense? I call it a jolly good idea.

SHAR. Splendid! By Jove, we'll carry it out too.

DUL. Indeed we won't. Jimmy, give me that list. (*Takes the subscription list from* JIMMY.) Mr. Fancourt will give me something, I'm sure.

FAN. I should be delighted, but (*nudging* SHAR-LAND) fact is, I've promised Sharland I wouldn't give anything except on the conditions Jimmy Stokes has just laid down.

DUL. Mr. Sharland.

SHAR. Very sorry, Miss Larondie, but fact is (*nudging* FANCOURT) I've promised Fancourt I wouldn't give anything except on the conditions Jimmy Stokes has laid down.

> (DULCIE *turns away indignantly, sees* LADY CRANDOVER *and* LADY CLARICE, *hesitates a moment, then goes somewhat defiantly to them.*)

DUL. Lady Crandover, may I beg you for a small subscription to Dick Ramsden's widow and children?

LADY CRAN. (*very coolly*). I always leave such things to Lord Crandover.   (*Turns away.*)

DUL. Perhaps Lady Clarice——

LADY CLAR. I thought I heard some one propose a way in which you could raise some money.

SIR BRICE (*coming from bar*).   Raise some money?
What's the matter here?

FAN.   Jimmy Stokes has just proposed that Miss
Larondie should benefit the Dick Ramsden fund by
selling a kiss by auction.

SIR BRICE.   What does Miss Larondie say?

DUL.   Impossible!

MON.   Not in the least.   If you will allow me,
gentlemen, I will constitute myself auctioneer.   (*To*
DULCIE.)   I beg you will place yourself entirely in
my hands, Miss Larondie.   Trust to my tact to bring
this affair to a most successful issue.   After all, it's
not so indelicate as slumming.

DUL.   No, no!

MON.   Allow me.   A rostrum.   That wine case.
(*A wine case is brought forward from side.*)   And that
barrel, if you please.   A hammer.   (*A large mallet,
such as is used for hammering bungs in beer barrels is
given to him.*)   Thank you.   (*He mounts.*)   Ladies
and gentlemen.   (*Chorus of "Hear, hear."*)   We must
all admit that the methods of raising the wind for all
sorts of worthless persons and useless charities stand
in need of entire revision.   Fancy fairs, amateur
theatricals, tableaux vivants, and such grotesque
futilities have had their day.   In the interests of those
long-suffering persons who get up charity entertain-
ments, and those yet more long-suffering persons who
attend them, it is high time to inaugurate a new
departure.   (*Cries of "Hear, hear."*)   Ladies and

gentlemen, there are three questions I take it which we ask ourselves when we raise a charitable subscription. Firstly, how shall we advertise ourselves, or amuse ourselves, as the case may be? Secondly, how far shall we be able to fleece our friends and the public? Thirdly, is the charity a deserving one?— The only really vital question of the three is "How shall we amuse ourselves in the sacred cause of charity?"   (*Cries of* "*Hear, hear.*")

LORD CRAN.   Lushington, stop this nonsense before it goes any further! Do you hear?

MON.   Ladies and gentlemen, I am in your hands. Shall I go on?

> (*Loud cries of* "*Yes, yes—Go on—Go on,*
> *Monty—Go on, Lushington.*")

LADY CRAN. (*to* LADY CLARICE).   Now she'll disgrace herself.

SIR BRICE (*having overheard*).   What did you say,. Lady Crandover?

LADY CRAN.   Nothing, Sir Brice.

SIR BRICE.   I understood you to say that Miss Larondie would disgrace herself.

DUL. (*with shame*).   Oh! Sir Brice, please let me go!

DAVID REMON *enters*. DULCIE *going off comes*
face to face with him—stops.

SIR BRICE.   No, stay. Don't take any notice of what has been said.

DAVID.   What has been said?

SIR BRICE. What business is it of yours? Miss Larondie is a connection of my family. Go on, Lushington—Go on. We'll have this auction—it's in the cause of charity, isn't it? Go on!

DAVID (*to* MONTAGU). What auction? What charity?

MON. (*soothingly*). Gentlemen, gentlemen, we are taking this far too seriously. Pray be calm and allow me to proceed. (*Cries of* "*Hear! Hear!—Go on, Monty!*") In an age when, as all good moralists lament, love is so often brought into the market, the marriage market—and other markets—and is sold to the highest bidder, it would, I am convinced, require a far more alarming outrage on propriety than that which we are now about to commit, to cause the now obsolete and unfashionable blush of shame to mount into the now obsolete and unfashionable cheek of modesty. Gentlemen, without further ado I offer for your competition—one kiss from Miss Larondie. (*Movement on the part of* DAVID. SIR BRICE *and he stand confronting each other.*) One kiss from Miss Larondie. What shall I say, gentlemen?

FAN. A sovereign.

MON. A sovereign is offered. I will on my own account advance ten shillings. Thirty shillings is offered, gentlemen.

SHAR. Thirty-five shillings.

MON. I cannot take an advance of less than ten shillings on this lot. Shall I say two pounds?

(SHARLAND *nods.*)

SIR BRICE.   A fiver.

(DAVID *steps forward towards* SIR BRICE.)

MON.   Thank you.   A fiver.   You are trifling, gentlemen.

FAN.   Six.

MON.   Six guineas—guineas only.   Six guineas is offered.   Gentlemen, if you do not bid up, in justice to my client I must withdraw the lot.

SHAR.   Seven.

SIR BRICE.   Ten.

MON.   Ten guineas.   Gentlemen, only ten guineas —only ten guineas for this rare and genuine, this highly desirable——

DAVID.   Twenty guineas.

MON.   Twenty guineas.   Thank you, sir.   This gentleman sees the quality of the article I am submitting——

SIR BRICE.   Thirty.

MON.   Thirty guineas.   Gentlemen, is the age of chivalry dead?   Mr. Fancourt, you are credited with some small amount of prowess among helpless ladies——

SHAR.   Cut in, Fan.

FAN.   Thirty-one.

MON.   Cannot take advances of less than five guineas.   Thirty-five guineas.   Gentlemen, will you force me to expatiate further on this exquisite——

DAVID.   Forty.

SIR BRICE.   Fifty.

(DAVID *and* SIR BRICE *are getting nearer to each other.*)

LORD CRAN.   Lushington, this is enough.   This is getting beyond a joke.

MON.   Then it's the only thing in life that ever did, so we'll continue.   Bid up, gentlemen, bid up.   I am assured, gentlemen, by my client, the vendor, that on no account will this lot ever be duplicated.   I am therefore offering you a unique opportunity of purchasing what I will venture to describe as the most——

DAVID.   Sixty.

SIR BRICE.   Seventy.

LORD CRAN.   Enough—enough !   Stop this jest.

MON.   Jest ?   I presume you are in earnest, gentlemen, about the purchase of this lot ?

DAVID.   I am.

SIR BRICE.   Go on, go on.

MON.   Seventy guineas, seventy guineas.   Gentlemen, you have not all done ?   Mr. Fancourt, faint heart——

SHAR.   Have another shy, Fan.

FAN.   Seventy-five.

MON.   Seventy-five.   Going at seventy-five guineas —the only chance ; going at seventy-five guineas.

FAN.   I say, Bricey, don't let me in.

SIR BRICE.   Eighty.   (*Looking at* DAVID.)

DAVID.   Ninety.

SIR BRICE.   A hundred.   (*Getting close to* DAVID.)

DAVID.   Two hundred.

SIR BRICE.   Three hundred.

LORD CRAN.   Skene, come away, do you hear? Come away.   (*Trying to drag* SIR BRICE *away.*)

SIR BRICE.   Let me be.   What's the last bidding, Lushington?

MON.   Three hundred guineas.

SIR BRICE.   Five.

DAVID.   A thousand.

SIR BRICE.   Fifteen hundred.

DAVID.   Two thousand.

SIR BRICE.   Three, and (*growling*) be damned to you!   (*Pause.*)   Knock it down, Lushington.

(*Long pause.*   DAVID *shows disappointment.*)

MON.   Three thousand guineas is offered, gentlemen.   (*Pause.*)   No further bid?   Going at three thousand guineas.   Going, going.   (*Knocks it down.*) Sir Brice, the lot is yours at three thousand guineas.

SIR BRICE.   Brinkler, pens, ink, and paper and a stamp.   (*Stepping towards barrel.*   DAVID *comes to him.*)   You've no further business here.

DAVID.   Yes, I think.

(*Pens, ink, and paper are brought to* SIR
        BRICE; *he hastily dashes off the cheque,
        gives it to* MONTAGU.)

MON.   Thank you.   Miss Larondie, a cheque for three thousand guineas.   You have secured an annuity for your *protégées*.

DUL. (*refusing the cheque*).   No.

D

SIR BRICE.   Miss Larondie.—(DAVID *looks at him.*)
It will perhaps save any further misconstruction if I
tell these ladies and gentlemen that an hour ago I
asked you to do me the honour to become my wife.

(*General surprise.*)

DUL.   Sir Brice——

SIR BRICE.   Will you do me the favour to take
that cheque for your charity, and the further favour
of becoming Lady Skene?

(MONTAGU *offers the cheque. A pause.* DULCIE
looks round, looks at LADY CLARICE,
takes the cheque.)

DUL.   Thank you, Sir Brice.   I shall be very
proud.

(DAVID *shows quiet despair. Goes to back.
Half the guests crowd round* SIR
BRICE *and* DULCIE, *congratulating. The
others show surprise, interest, and amaze-
ment.*)

LADY CRAN. (*in a very loud voice*).   My carriage at
once.

LORD CRAN. (*in a low voice to her*).   We'd better
stay and make the best of it.

LADY CRAN.   No, my carriage.   Come, Clarice.
(*Goes off. A good many of the guests follow her.*)

(*Exeunt* LADY CLARICE *and* LORD CRANDOVER.)

SIR BRICE (*to* FANCOURT).   The Crandovers have
gone off in a huff.   Bet you a tenner they'll dine
with me before three months.

FAN. Done!

(*The band strikes up. A general movement of those who remain towards the ball-room.*)

SIR BRICE (*to* DULCIE). If you will allow me, I will place you in my sister's care. She's in the ball-room.

DUL. (*looking at her dress*). No, Sir Brice, not yet. I've one of my old evening dresses upstairs. May I put it on?

SIR BRICE. Yes, if you like. I'll wait for you at the ball-room door.

DUL. I won't be a moment.

(*Running off with great excitement and delight. All the guests move towards the ball-room.*)

MON. (*to* SIR BRICE). Congratulate you heartily, Sir Brice. (*Offering hand.*)

SIR BRICE (*taking it*). Oh, I suppose it's all right.

CHAR. (*to* SIR BRICE). Your wooing was charmingly fresh and original, Sir Brice.

SIR BRICE. Think so? (*Turns away.*)

CHAR. (*to* MONTY). What on earth does he want to marry the girl for?

MON. Somebody has bet him a guinea he wouldn't.

(*Exeunt* CHARLEY *and* MONTAGU *into the ball-room.*)

FAN. Bravo, Bricey, my boy! This'll make up to you for losing the Leger.

SIR BRICE. Think so? I'll go and get a smoke outside. (*Exit at gates.*)

SHAR. (*to* FANCOURT).   Just like Bricey to do a silly fool's trick like this.

FAN.   I pity the girl.   Bricey will make a sweet thing in husbands.

SHAR.   By Jove, yes.   Her life 'll be a regular beno, and no mistake.

(*Exeunt into ball-room.   DAVID is left alone sitting at back.*)

Enter EDDIE.   DAVID *drinks and laughs rather bitterly to himself.*

EDDIE.   What's gone wrong, Davy?

DAVID.   Miss Larondie is going to marry Sir Brice Skene.

EDDIE.   Oh, then the solar system is all out of joint!   Poor old big brother!

DAVID.   I won't feel it, Eddie, I won't feel it.

EDDIE.   Yes, you will, Davy.   Yes, you will.   Why weren't you tumbled into Mars, or Jupiter, or Saturn, or into any world but this?

DAVID.   Why?

EDDIE.   This is the very worst world that ever spun round, for a man who has a heart.   Look at all the heartless and stupid people; what a paradise this is for them!

DAVID.   I'll forget her and plunge into my work. There are millions of new worlds to discover.

EDDIE.   Yes, but are they all like this? because if they are, what's the use of discovering millions more of them? Oh, Davy, isn't there one perfect world out of all the millions—just one—where everything goes right, and fiddles never play out of tune?

DAVID. There isn't one, Eddie, not one of all the millions. They're all alike.

EDDIE. And breaking hearts in all of them? Oh, let's pretend there's just one perfect star somewhere, shall we?

DAVID. Oh, very well; let's pretend there's one in the nebula of Andromeda. It's a long way off, and it does no harm to pretend. Besides, it makes the imbroglio of the universe complete if there is one perfect world somewhere in it.

SIR BRICE *enters smoking, throws away his cigarette, looks at* DAVID *rather insolently, goes into the ballroom.*

DAVID (*starts up*). If he doesn't treat her well— (*goes after him, stops, comes back*)—what does it matter? It's all a farce, but if he doesn't treat her well, I feel, Eddie, I could put a murder into the farce, just for fun.

EDDIE. Come home, Davy.

DAVID. Let me be, my boy. It's only a pinprick. I shall get over it. ˊ

EDDIE. I wish I could bear it for you, Davy.

DAVID. That would only mean your heart breaking instead of mine.

EDDIE.   Don't you think I'd break my heart for you, Davy?

DUL. (*her voice heard off*).   Thanks! I can't wait! Sir Brice is waiting for me!

EDDIE.   Poor old big brother!   (*Exit.*)

Enter DULCIE *down the stairs in evening dress, excited, radiant.*

DUL. (*seeing* DAVID).   I thought you'd gone.   Did you hear?   I'm to be Lady Skene.   Do I look nice? (*Very excited.*)   I beg your pardon—I don't know what I'm saying.   (*Looks round.*)   I wish there was a looking-glass here.   I wonder where Sir Brice is— I'm to be Lady Skene—won't you congratulate me?

DAVID.   I hope you will be happy.

DUL.   No, congratulate me.

DAVID.   I hope you will be happy.

DUL.   Ah, you think I shan't be happy?   Then I will, just to spite you!

DAVID.   Ah, do spite me and be happy.

DUL. (*fidgeting with her dress*).   I'm sure my dress isn't right.   Wasn't that a jest about the kiss?

DAVID.   A great jest.

DUL.   You wouldn't have really given two thousand guineas for a kiss from me?

DAVID (*nods*).   Why not?   Sir Brice gave fifty thousand for the pleasure of losing the Leger.

DUL.   But he stood to win.

DAVID. So did I.

DUL. What?

DAVID. The kiss.

DUL. But you wouldn't really have given two thousand guineas for it?

DAVID (*nods*). I think highly of women. It's a pleasing delusion of mine. Don't disturb it.

DUL. (*looking at him, after a little pause*). You are the strangest creature, but what a splendid friend you'd make! I'm keeping Sir Brice waiting. (*Turns round, sees that the lace on the skirt of her dress is hanging loose.*) Look at that lace! What can I do? (*Giving him a pin.*) Would you mind pinning that lace on my skirt?

DAVID (*takes the pin, kneels, and pins the lace*). Will that do?

DUL. Thank you so much. Do I look nice?

(*He looks up at her imploringly, like a dumb creature ; she glances swiftly round to see that they are alone, suddenly bends and kisses him ; runs up the ball-room steps. A burst of dance-music.*)

(*Three years and a half pass between Acts I. and II.*)

ACT II

A great crowd in farther room. Discover Lady Crandover, Lady Clarice, Charley Wishanger (*now*
Lady Shalford), Montagu, Fancourt, Sharland, *and the young men of the first Act. Among
the guests in farther room* Sir Winchmore Wills
and the Hon. Percy Blanchflower.

Lady Crandover (*looking off*). It's astounding.

Char. What is?

Lady Cran. The way every one runs after this
woman. She's got everybody here again to-night.

Lady Clar. Professor Rawkinson and the Bishop
of Malmesbury were fighting to get her an ice.

Char. What is the secret of her popularity?

Mon. Why did you come here to-night?

Char. I? Oh, I came because everybody else
comes. Why did you?

Mon. Because everybody else comes. Do we
ever have any other reason for going anywhere,

admiring anything, saying anything, or doing anything? The secret of getting a crowd to your
rooms is, " Entice a bell-wether." The flock will
follow.

CHAR. Who was bell-wether to Lady Skene?

MON. The old Duchess of Norwich.

LADY CRAN. I suppose the duchess knows all
about Lady Skene's antecedents?

MON. What does it matter about anybody's
antecedents to-day?

LADY CRAN. We must draw the line somewhere.

MON. On the contrary, my dear Lady Crandover,
we must *not* draw the line *anywhere*. We have yet
got to learn what democracy means.

LADY CLAR. What does democracy mean?

MON. That there is no line to be drawn, either
socially, morally, pecuniarily, politically, religiously,
or anywhere.

LADY CLAR. How horrid! (*Turns away.*)

MON. (*continuing*). Who are the interesting
people here to-night? Of course there's a crowd of
respectable nonentities—But who are the attractions?
Attraction number one: a financier's wife — the
most charming woman in the world—gives the very
best dinners in London—had an extensive acquaint-
ance amongst the officers at Aldershot fifteen years
ago.

THE HON. PERCY BLANCHFLOWER, *a fussy, buzzy, mincing, satirical little creature, with a finicking, feminine manner and gestures, has overheard, comes up to the group.*

BLAN. What's this?—eh?—hum? No scandal, I trust?

MON. No, Blanchflower; no scandal—only the plain, unvarnished truth about all our friends.

BLAN. Ah, then I'll stay and listen. Go on!

MON. Attraction number two: leading temperance and social purity orator—can move an audience of ten thousand to tears—leads the loosest of lives—and is suspected of having poisoned his wife.

BLAN. But she had a fearful cockney accent. And he's very kind to his aged aunt and pretty niece—eh?—hum? Give him his due.

MON. My dear Blanchflower, I'm not blaming the man for poisoning his wife. It may have been a necessity of his position; and if she had a cockney accent, it was a noble thing to do. Attraction number three: pretty little lady who has just emerged triumphantly from the Divorce Court, without a spot upon her pretty little character. Attraction number four——

(LADY CLARICE *rejoins the group.*)

EDDIE *enters from conservatory, and without joining group is near enough to hear what is being said.*

BLAN. (*interrupting*). No! No! Skip number

four! We know all about her. Attraction number five! And mind, I shall thoroughly scold you all— when Lushington has got through his list.

MON. (*proceeding*). Attraction number five: impressionist artist, novelist, and general dirty modern dabbler — is consummately clever — a consistent scoundrel in every relation of life—especially to women—a liar, a cheat, a drunkard—and a great personal friend of my own.

BLAN. Oh, this is too shocking! This is really too shocking!

LADY CLAR. You've ómitted the chief attraction to-night—our famous astronomer.

(EDDIE *shows increased attention.*)

MON. Remon?

BLAN. Of course. Since his great discovery we've only one astronomer in England.

CHAR. What was his great discovery?

BLAN. Don't know. Some new spots on Venus, I believe.

MON. No. That she wanted a new belt to hide the manners of her inhabitants, which were distinctly visible through his new large telescope, and if constantly observed would tend to the corruption of London society.

BLAN. You naughty person! You're not to look through that telescope!

MON. My dear Blanchflower, I have; and I assure you we have nothing to fear. But I tremble for the morals of Venus if they get a telescope as large as Remon's and begin to look at us.

BLAN.   Tell me, this friendship of the astronomer with Lady Skene—eh? hum?—quite innocent—eh?

MON.   I have never known any friendship between a man and a married woman that was not innocent. How can it be guilty, unless the woman is ugly?

LADY CLAR.   Poor dear Lady Skene is fearfully ill-used, I hear. (SIR WINCHMORE WILLS, *a fashionable middle-aged physician, comes up and joins the group.*) I've heard that Sir Brice gets drunk and—then—dreadful things happen.

BLAN.   But that can't be true—eh? hum?—Sir Winchmore—eh?

SIR WIN.   I have never treated Sir Brice for alcoholism, nor Lady Skene for bruises.

BLAN.   No, of course, no—but you've heard—hum? eh?

SIR WIN.   Singularly enough, I have never heard or seen anything in the least discreditable to any one of my patients.

CHAR.   I know for a fact Sir Brice came a terrific cropper last week at Epsom, and doesn't know how he stands.   (EDDIE *is listening attentively.*)

BLAN.   And—hum—the astronomer—hum? eh? hum?—is there any truth—eh?

MON. Well, we *know* that our astronomer succeeded a few months ago to an immense fortune left him by a mountaineering friend in Canada. We *know* that Sir Brice neglects his wife and is practically ruined. We *know* that Lady Skene continues her parties, her household, her carriages, and we *know* that our astronomer pays (*long pause*) the greatest attentions to Lady Skene. Of course this doesn't absolutely prove Lady Skene's guilt—yet why should we deprive ourselves of the pleasure of believing and circulating a spicy story about our friends merely because there is only the very slightest foundation for it?

(EDDIE *rises rather indignantly and comes a little nearer to the group without being noticed by them.*)

BLAN. Oh, this is very naughty of us. We are actually talking scandal about our hostess. We ought to be ashamed of ourselves!

LADY CRAN. Really, it's time somebody made a stand, or society will be ruined. Here is a woman who was actually a barmaid at a public-house—her name is in everybody's mouth in connection with this astronomer, and yet——

MON. And yet we crush to her receptions. At least you do, Lady Crandover.

LADY CRAN. Oh, we are all to blame for lowering the moral tone of society as we are doing.

BLAN. Oh, my dear Lady Crandover, please, please, please, do not make things unpleasant by dragging in morality. But where is the astronomer? —eh? hum?

EDDIE. My brother will be coming by and by. I'll tell him he's wanted here.

> (*Exit.* BLANCHFLOWER *looks aghast and stares round' at all the rest, who show some slight discomfiture.* FANCOURT *and* SHARLAND *join the group.*)

BLAN. Dear me! That's the astronomer's brother. Have we said anything?—hum? eh?

MON. My dear Blanchflower, what does it matter what lies we tell about each other when none of our friends think any the worse of us if they are true!

BLAN. Oh, but it's very wrong to tell lies, very wrong indeed. I've not seen Sir Brice to-night. Where is he? eh?

FAN. Bricey doesn't generally stay very long at his wife's receptions.

SHAR. Bricey's latest little hobby is teaching the girls at the Folly Theatre to box.

FAN. Yes. Last Tuesday he was in great force at the Ducks and Drakes Club egging on Betty Vignette to fight Sylvia Vernon.

SHAR. Oh, that's coming off—two hundred a side, on Sunday night week.

FAN. (*cautiously winking at* SHARLAND, *in a warning way*). I say, old chap, keep it quiet. I wonder where Bricey is to-night.

MON. What does it matter whether he is playing baccarat with the pot-boy at the corner, or clandestinely taking his nurse-girl to the Alhambra on the pretence that it is a missionary meeting? We may be quite sure that Bricey is doing something equally vicious, stupid, disreputable, and—original.

CHAR. (*to* MONTY). Come here, you monster. Have you heard the news?

> (*During the conversation of* CHARLEY *and* MONTY *the other group put their heads together and whisper.*)

MON. What?

CHAR. Sir Joseph is going to leave the March-moor estates to Clarice.

MON. (*glancing at* LADY CLARICE). Sure?

CHAR. Fact. The will is to be signed in a few days. Clarice told me so in confidence.

MON. Thanks.

> (*Strolls cautiously up to* LADY CLARICE, *hovers about her till he gets a chance of speaking to her. A general laugh from the group.*)

BLAN. (*who has been in centre of group*). Oh, this is very shocking! We are actually talking scandal about our host. And he has his good points. He hasn't strangled his baby, has he, Sir Winchmore?

SIR WIN. Sir Brice has the greatest consideration for the welfare of his offspring. (DULCIE *comes from other room magnificently dressed, restless, pale, nervous, excited.*) He never goes near it.

> (*An awkward little pause as they see* DULCIE. LADY CLARICE *goes up to her.*)

LADY CLAR. What a lot of interesting folks you

always have, dear. (*Looking off through eye-glass.*)
Who is that lady in pale blue?

DUL. Mrs. Chalmers.

LADY CLAR. The lady who has figured so much
in the newspapers lately? What a singular gift you
have of attracting all sorts of people, dear.

DUL. Have I? That's sometimes a misfortune.

LADY CLAR. Yes, it does involve one in undesir-
able acquaintances and relationships.

DUL. Still it must be rather annoying to be without
it. (*Goes restlessly to* SIR WINCHMORE. LADY
CLARICE *shows slight mortification.*
MONTY, *who has been watching the scene,
goes up to her.*)

MON. Lady Clarice, let me give you some supper.
(*Takes her off.*)

DUL. (*taking* SIR WINCHMORE *a little aside*). Sir
Winchmore—so kind of you to come. (*In a half
whisper.*) That sleeping draught's no use—you must
send me a stronger one.

SIR WIN. (*shakes his head*). Lady Skene——

DUL. (*impetuously*). Yes, yes, please—I must
have it—I've not slept for three nights.

SIR WIN. Lady Skene, let me beg you——

DUL. No, no, no,—you must patch me up and
keep me going somehow till the end of the season,
then you shall do what you like with me.

SIR WIN. But, Lady Skene——

DUL. (*intense suppressed nervousness*). But——(*Im-

ploringly.)   Oh, don't contradict me.—When any one speaks to me I feel I must shriek out "Yah, yah, yah!" (BLANCHFLOWER *has been following her up and has overheard the last speech.* DULCIE *sees that* BLANCHFLOWER *is looking at her, controls herself after an immense effort, puts on society smile. To* BLANCH-FLOWER.) The bishop was talking to me just now about his mission to convert the West End of London, and I could scarcely keep from shrieking out to him "Yah, yah, yah!" Isn't it strange?

BLAN.   Not at all.   Clergymen always produce that effect upon me.

DUL. (*turning to* SIR WINCHMORE). Sir Winchmore, you'll run up to the nursery and see Rosy before you go, won't you?

SIR WIN.   What's the matter?

DUL.   Nothing, only a little tumble and a bruise. My sister Nell is with her, but you'll just see her?

SIR WIN.   Certainly.

DUL.   I'm so foolish about her. (*Imploringly.*) She is strong and healthy, isn't she?

SIR WIN.   A magnificent child.   ·

SIR BRICE *has entered through other room. He looks coarser and more dissipated than in first Act, and is more brutalised. There is a slight movement of all the guests away from him.*

DUL. (*not seeing* SIR BRICE. *To* SIR WINCHMORE). Really?   Really?

E

SIR WIN. Really. Sir Brice and you may well be proud of her.

(SIR BRICE'S *entrance has caused an awkward pause amongst the guests.*)

SIR WIN. We were talking of your youthful daughter, Sir Brice.

SIR BRICE. I hate brats.

(*Another awkward pause.*)

DUL. (*to cover it, rattles away with forced gaiety*). We shall see you at Ascot, of course, Mr. Blanchflower. —Sir Winchmore, what are these frightful new waters that you are sending all your patients to?—That reminds me, Lady Shalford, how is Sir Digby's gout?

(*Slight continued movement of the guests away from* SIR BRICE.)

CHAR. Terrible. I pack him off to Aix on Thursday.

DUL. (*same tone*). So sorry he couldn't come to-night.

CHAR. My dear, I'm very glad, and so I'm sure is everybody who knows him. If Aix doesn't cure him, I shall try something drastic.

SIR BRICE (*comes a little nearer, slight instinctive repulsion of all*). Serve him as I did my trainer Burstow.

DUL. (*noticing the guests' repulsion, slightly frowns at* SIR BRICE *unobserved by the guests, and goes on speaking to change the subject*). We shall go to Homburg again——

SIR BRICE (*speaks her down. To* CHARLEY). Burstow had the gout. I treated him myself. (*Coarse little chuckle.*) I gave him a bottle of port, champagne at intervals, and brown brandy *ad lib.* A tombstone now marks Burstow's precise position, which is longitudinal. I wrote his epitaph, but the vicar wouldn't pass it. So the vicar and I have a law-suit on.

> (*Another coarse little chuckle. Another awkward little pause.*)

DUL. (*to cover it, continues*). Mr. Fancourt, did you make inquiries about the house-boat for us?

SIR BRICE. We shan't go to Henley.

DUL. (*to* FANCOURT). Then of course you needn't make inquiries.

FAN. But I've arranged it. My brother will be awfully delighted if you'll accept the loan of his for the Henley week. You and Sir Brice will be awfully pleased with it.

SIR BRICE (*more decidedly*). We shall not go to Henley.

DUL. (*another covered frown at* SIR BRICE, *again controlling herself with immense effort and speaking very calmly*). Will you thank your brother and say we shall not be going.

> (*Awkward pause.* SIR BRICE *puts his hands in his pockets and yawns.* DULCIE *engages the group in conversation, and they crowd round her.*)

SIR BRICE. Sharland, come and have a little game of poker in the smoking-room.

SHAR. Very sorry, Bricey, haven't so much as a fiver with me.

SIR BRICE. You can borrow. Can't you borrow, eh ?

SHAR.   Very sorry, dear old chap ; never borrow or lend.   (*Goes back to* DULCIE's *group—they are talking in an interested way.* SIR BRICE *stands and yawns, looks sulky and vicious, then calls out.*)

SIR BRICE.   Fancourt. (FANCOURT *glances but does not come.*)   Fan—Fan, I say——(*At length* FANCOURT *comes.*)   We're getting up a little hand at poker just to wind up this infernally dull evening.

FAN. (*shakes his head and laughs*).   Not good enough, Bricey—not good enough.

REMON *enters.   At his entrance guests show marked interest, and the conversation stops.* SIR BRICE *watches with a sulky expression.* DULCIE *shows great pleasure, goes to meet* REMON.

DUL.   I'm so glad you've come.   You have so many engagements.

DAVID.   None more pleasing than this.

BLAN.   I insist on knowing Mr. Remon—somebody introduce me—introduce me.

DUL.   Mr. Remon—Mr. Percy Blanchflower.

BLAN.   I'm so delighted to know you.   We want to look through that large telescope of yours.

DAVID.   It's in the South of France.

BLAN.   I go there every winter.   We were talking about your wonderful discoveries—hum ? eh ?   We want to know all about them.

DAVID.   Oh, spare me, or rather, yourselves.

(SIR BRICE *laughs*.)

FAN.   You seem to have got something good all to yourself, Bricey.

SIR BRICE.   Yes, I have.   (*Laughs*.)

BLAN. (*aside, to* SIR WINCHMORE).   What is Remon's discovery? eh?

SIR WIN.   Haven't the least idea—something about Saturn, I fancy.

BLAN. (*buzzes up to* REMON).   Your last discovery now—about Saturn, wasn't it—hum? eh?

> (*All through* DAVID'S *conversation with the guests, he adopts the same light, frivolous tone throughout, and speaks without the least suggestion of seriousness. This gives a contrast to the scenes with* DULCIE.)

DAVID (*amused, very light and chaffing tone*).   About Saturn?   Oh yes.   My conjecture is that bad folks when they die are sent to Saturn to study current theology, and if at the end of five hundred years they know anything about it, their probation is complete.

(*General laugh.*   DAVID *turns to group.*   SIR BRICE *laughs*.)

FAN.   What is it, Bricey?

SIR BRICE.   Lady Skene is making a howling fuss with all of you to-night.   She'll make a howling fuss of another kind next week.   I can't stand that astronomer fellow.

(*Goes up to* DULCIE *and group and listens*.)

BLAN. But do tell us, Lady Skene, what is Mr. Remon's great speciality—hum? eh?

DUL. I believe Mr. Remon has devoted a great deal of time to the study of sun-spots.

BLAN. Oh—ah, yes—hum. Now (*to* DAVID) what is the special function of sun-spots—hum? eh? What do they do?

DAVID (*still amused, chaffing, mysterious*). I've long had a suspicion that there is a very subtle connection between sun-spots and politics—in fact, I am convinced that the present decadence of political manners and morals is entirely caused by the persistence of a certain sun-spot. As soon as we can remove it, the natural ingrained honesty and patriotism of our politicians will reassert themselves.

(*General laugh.*)

SIR BRICE (*pushes a little forward with a rather insolent manner to* DAVID). My character is always puzzling me. Can you tell me whether its present development is due to sun-spots?

DAVID (*is about to reply rather angrily, is checked by a look from* DULCIE, *speaks very politely*). You might not think me polite, Sir Brice.

SIR BRICE (*persisting*). I should like to have a scientific examination made of my character.

DAVID (*still controlling himself*). I fear I should not make a sympathetic operator.

SIR BRICE (*still persisting*). But——

DUL. (*who has been watching very apprehensively, to*

SIR BRICE). My dear, Lady Franklin wants to ask you something about a horse for Ascot. She was here a moment ago. (*Looking around, drawing* SIR BRICE *away from the group, who close up round* REMON. DULCIE *is getting* SIR BRICE *away.*) For God's sake keep away from us! (*A guest is just passing,* DULCIE *turns to her with a forced society smile and manner.*) How do you do? What a sweet frock! (*Shakes hands with guest, who passes on.*)

SIR BRICE (*sulkily*). What's the matter?
(*Approaching her.*)

DUL. Don't go near any one. You smell of brandy.
(*All this under breath with great terror and apprehension.*)

SIR BRICE (*getting a little nearer her*). I rather like the smell of brandy.

DUL. (*terrified, under breath*). Keep away—keep away—if you come a step nearer to me I shall shriek out before everybody. You nearly drove me out of my mind this morning. Oh, for Heaven's sake—do go—do go!

SIR BRICE. Well, as it's infernally slow here I will go—but—you may as well know, there will be no Ascot, no Henley, no Goodwood, no Homburg, no anything. We shall be sold up within a month.

DUL. (*is staggering for a moment*).

SIR BRICE. Ta ta!—my blessing—I'm going to the Club.

(*Exit.* DULCIE *stands overwhelmed for a*

moment, tries to pull herself together, staggers a little. DAVID, *who has been watching her and* SIR BRICE, *leaves the group and comes to her, speaks with great feeling, very softly, his tone and manner to her in great contrast to his tone and manner with the guests.*)

DAVID.   Lady Skene, you are in trouble—you are ill.

DUL. (*again with the forced society smile*).   No, only the fatigue of the season, and the rooms are so crowded, aren't they?

(*A group of guests begin little gestures and significant glances and whispers, watching* DAVID *and* DULCIE.)

EDDIE *re-enters, and unnoticed looks from one group to the other.*

DAVID.   I'll tell Sir Winchmore.

DUL.   No, don't take any notice.   If I can only get through this evening!   (*With a sudden instinct, appealing to him with great entreaty.*)   Tell me something that will carry me through this next hour till they have all gone.   Give me that sort of medicine!

DAVID (*with the utmost tenderness and feeling, in a low voice, bending over her.   The glances and whispers continue*).   Your trouble isn't real.   This society world of yours isn't a real world.   There's one little star in Andromeda where everything is real.   You've wandered down here amongst these shadows when you should have stayed at home.

DUL. (*pleased, lending herself to his suggestion*). Aren't these real men and women?

DAVID. No. They are only masquerading. Good God, I think we are all masquerading! Look at them! If you touched them with reality they would vanish. And so with your trouble of to-night. Fly back to Andromeda, and you will see what a dream all this is.

DUL. How strange! I was half dead a moment ago, and you've made me so well and happy. But you—do you belong to Andromeda,—or to this world?

(EDDIE *has been watching and comes down near to them.*)

DAVID. To both. But the little star in Andromeda is my home. I'm only wandering with you amongst these phantoms.

(*They have become for the moment quite absorbed.*
EDDIE, *who has been watching the whispers and smiles, comes up to them, speaks rather sharply.*)

EDDIE. Lady Skene—that lamp-shade—(*pointing off*). Won't it catch fire? (*Taking* DAVID'S *arm, dragging him away.*) I want to talk to you, Davy.

(DULCIE *turns to manservant, points to the lamp-shade, and gives him directions concerning it.*)

DAVID (*turns savagely on* EDDIE, *growls*). Why the devil did you come between us?

EDDIE.   Don't you care for her, Davy?

DAVID.   Care for her?

> (DULCIE *having given manservant instructions,*
> *goes to guests.*)

EDDIE.   Do you know what these folks are saying?
That Sir Brice is ruined, and that you have lately
come into a fortune.

DAVID.   Well?

EDDIE.   And that she continues her parties, her
dresses, her house, because you——

> (*Stops, looks at* DAVID.)

DAVID (*looks round at guests savagely.   Stands
for a moment or two reflecting, his face then assumes a
look of great resolve*).

EDDIE (*watching him*).   I was right to tell you,
Davy?

DAVID (*shakes* EDDIE'S *hand in reply.   Another
little pause*).   Go and tell her, Eddie, that I must see
her for a few minutes by and by—to-night—when
everybody is gone.

EDDIE.   What are you going to do, Davy?

DAVID.   We'll get away south to-morrow, old boy.
The observatory's nearly finished, and—there's no
tittle-tattle between the snows and the stars.   Go and
tell her I must see her, and bring me back her answer.

> (EDDIE *goes to* DULCIE, *who is talking to guests.*
> *A general movement of guests towards*
> REMON.   *They group round him again.*
> *Guests are seen being introduced to him.*)

EDDIE (*to* DULCIE). You've not been down to supper, Lady Skene.

DULCIE. I really don't want any.

EDDIE. But I've a message for you.

DULCIE. A message?

EDDIE. From Andromeda.

> (*Exeunt* DULCIE *and* EDDIE.)

Re-enter MONTY *with* LADY CLARICE, *evidently on very good terms.*

LADY CLAR. You are really too dreadful.

> (*Leaves him, and joins* LADY CRANDOVER. MONTY *goes up to group of* REMON *and guests.*)

BLAN. (*buzzing round* REMON). That's a charming theory of yours about the effect of sun-spots on morality.

DAVID. Yes. It isn't true, but it's very consoling. That's why I invented it.

MON. If it's charming and consoling, why should it be true?

DAVID. Why should it? and put everything else out of focus.

BLAN. Out of focus! Ah! I'm afraid you're a dreadful, dreadful pessimist.

DAVID. No; but I'm as willing to play that part as any other, since it's only in jest.

CHAR. In jest? What do you mean?

DAVID. I have to spend so much time alone amongst the stars, that when I come back into the world I am quite at a loss. I find myself amongst crowds of shadows—very charming shadows they are —playing at money-making, playing at religion, playing at love, at art, at politics, at all sorts of odd games, and so for the time I join in the game, and pretend to take an interest in it; and a very pleasant game it is, so long as we don't mistake it for reality.

CHAR. But surely we are realities!

DAVID. With the profoundest respect in the world, Lady Shalford, I cannot bring myself to believe that you are. Still, I won't spoil your game by staying out.

BLAN. (*with a little affected, mincing earnestness*). Oh, but surely, surely there is Something real Somewhere. Oh, yes—surely, surely—we must believe that there is—hum? eh?—a Kind of—eh?—a Sort of a Something—Somewhere, eh?

DAVID. If you like to believe there is a kind of a sort of a something—somewhere—and you find it consoling, I'm as willing to pretend to believe that as anything else.

BLAN. (*still with the same affected earnestness*). Oh, but surely, when you look into your own heart— hum? eh?——

DAVID. I always wear a mask over my heart. I never dare look into it.

Re-enter EDDIE.

MONTY. I find this world a remarkably comfortable and well-arranged place. I always do exactly as I like. If I want anything I buy it, whether I pay for it or no. If I see a woman I admire I make love to her, whether she belongs to another man or no. If a lie will answer my purpose, I tell it. I can't remember I ever denied myself one single pleasure in life; nor have I ever put myself out to oblige a fellow-creature. I am consistently selfish, and I find it pays; I credit everybody else with the same consistent selfishness, and I am never deceived in my estimate of character. These are my principles, and I always act up to them. And I assure you I find this world the pleasantest possible place.

DAVID. A fairy palace! An enchanted spot! Only take care! While you are dancing, there may be a volcano underneath.

MON. If there is, surely dancing is the pleasantest preparation for the general burst-up.

EDDIE. Davy——

DAVID (*goes to him*). Well?

EDDIE. She'll see you to-night. Come back here when they've all gone.

BLAN. (*to* MONTY). How charmingly frank you are, Monty.

MON. Why not? We have one supreme merit in this generation—we have ceased to render to virtue the homage of hypocrisy.

DAVID. And our moral evolution is now complete. Good-night!

(*Exeunt* DAVID *and* EDDIE.)

LADY CLARICE *re-enters.* MONTY *joins her. The group breaks up.*

MON. (*coming down with* LADY CLARICE). Of course I know there is something wretchedly philistine and provincial about marriage, but I will take care this aspect of it is never presented to you.

LADY CLAR. I wonder what makes marriage so unlovely and so uninteresting?

MON. The exaggerated notion that prevails of its duties and responsibilities. Once do away with that, and it becomes an ideal state. Lady Clarice, you'd find me the most agreeable partner in the world.

LADY CLAR. You'd be like most other husbands, I suppose.

MON. No; I should be unique. Husbands, as a rule, are foolish, jealous brutes, who insist that men shall have all the rights and women all the duties,—men shall have all the sweets and women all the sours of the marriage state. We would start on an entirely new plan. The sours we would naturally equally avoid, and the sweets,—if there are any,—we would naturally do our best to secure.

LADY CLAR. Separately, or together?

MON. According to our tastes. If you do me the honour to accept me, I pledge you my word I will never have the offensively bad taste to speak of a husband's rights. There shall be no "lord and master" nonsense.

LADY CLAR. It sounds very well in theory. I wonder how it would work.

MON. Let us try. If we succeed we shall solve the vexed question of the age, and make ourselves happy in showing mankind the road to happiness.

LADY CLAR. But if we fail?

MON. We shall have sacrificed ourselves for the benefit of our species. But we can't fail, the plan is perfect.

LADY CLAR. If I spoke of rights and duties—if I were jealous——

MON. Ah! then you would be departing from the plan. Its charm is that it is a patent, self-adjusting, self-repairing, safety-valve plan, with double escapement action suited to all climates and dispositions. No rights, no duties, no self-assertion, no quarrels, no jealousy.

LADY CLAR. And no love?

MON. Love is a perverted animal instinct, which is really a great bar to solid happiness in marriage. Believe me, you will like me and respect me in the end for not pretending to any such outworn impulses. You see I am frank.

LADY CLAR. You are indeed. (*Looking at him very closely, watching him.*) You know—(*pause*)—my father cannot make any great settlements, and— (*watching him closely*) I have no expectations.

MON. (*stands it without flinching*). So I am aware. I'm frightfully in debt, and I have no expectations.

But there is a house in Grosvenor Place—it would suit us exactly.

LADY CLAR. (*watching him*). But — without money?

MON. I cannot afford to be economical. I have acted on that principle throughout life, and I have always had the very best of everything. I do not see we need change it.

LADY CLAR. You are perfectly atrocious—I don't care for you in the least.

MON. (*with great politeness*). My plan is precisely adapted to such cases.

(LADY CRANDOVER *appears at back.*)

LADY CRAN. Come, Clarice—everybody is going.
(*Exit.*)

MON. I shall call on Lord Crandover to-morrow. You don't speak. Does silence give consent?

LADY CLAR. I can't help your calling.
(*Exit.* MONTY *stands in slight deliberation.* CHARLEY *comes out from the conservatory behind him. She has been watching the last part of the scene from the conservatory.*)

CHAR. Well?

MON. Landed, I think. You're sure about Sir Joseph and the estate?

CHAR. Quite. But it's not to be known yet. I'm a pet, ain't I?

MON. You are.   (*Kisses her hand.*)

CHAR. I must be going. That creature at home will be raising furies.

MON. When do you pack him to Aix?

CHAR. Thursday, praise the Lord!

MON. When shall I call?

CHAR. Friday?

MON. What time?

CHAR. Come to lunch?

MON. Yes.

CHAR. Friday at two. (*Exchange looks full of meaning.*) Bye-bye.

MON. Bye-bye.

> (*During the last scene* DULCIE *has come on and has been seen saying good-night to the last guests in the other room.*)

CHAR. Oh dear, am I the last? Good-bye, dear. (*Kisses* DULCIE.) Monty, come and see me to my carriage.

MON. Good-bye, Lady Skene.

DUL. Good-bye.

> (*Exit* MONTY *with* CHARLEY. *Manservant appears at back seeing to lamps.*)

DUL. (*to* Servant). Thomson, I expect Mr. Remon. Show him in here.

SERV. Yes, my lady.

> (*Exit.* HELEN *appears at outer door still in nurse's costume.*)

HELEN (*peeps in*). They have all gone, dear.

DUL. (*staggers up to* HELEN, *throws her arms round*

F

her).   I've got such a fever, Nell.   Put your nice cold hand on my forehead.   That's right.   Hold it tight—tight.   Why didn't you dress and come into my party ?

HELEN.   I was so tired and bored at the last, and I wanted to be with Rosy.

DUL.   She's all right ?

HELEN.   Yes.   She was awake a moment ago.

DUL. (*suddenly*).   Fetch her !   I must see her ! Oh, you're right, Nell; it's been a hateful evening, with only one bright spot in it—when he came and whispered something so sweet.

HELEN (*suddenly*).   Dulcie, you're sure of yourself?

DUL.   I'm sure of him.

HELEN.   He has never spoken—of—of——

DUL.   Of love ?   Never.   What does that matter? I know he loves me.

HELEN.   Dulcie, you shouldn't say that—even to yourself.

DUL.   Oh, that's all nonsense, Nell; as if there was ever a woman in this world that didn't know when she was loved !

HELEN.   Dulcie !

DUL. (*provokingly*).   He loves me !   He loves me !   He loves me, and I'm not ashamed of it, and I don't care who knows it.   (*Throwing her arms round* HELEN'S *neck.*)   Nell, I'm so happy.

HELEN.   Why ?

DUL.   Brice says we are utterly ruined; it's no

more than I've guessed for months.   We're ruined, but I won't feel it to-night.   I'll feel it to-morrow. I'll be happy for one minute to-night.   He is coming.

HELEN.   Mr. Remon?

DUL.   Yes.   Don't look shocked, Nell.   Listen; this is true.   Mr. Remon and I have never said one word to each other that all the world might not have heard.   (*Pause.*)   I'm glad all the world hasn't heard it though.

(Servant *comes in, announces* MR. REMON.)

DUL.   (*to* HELEN).   Go and fetch Rosy.   Yes! Yes!

(*Exit* HELEN.   DAVID *has entered;* Servant *has gone off.*)

(*To* DAVID.)   I'm so glad you've come.   I want you to see Rosy.   She's awake.   You've never seen her.

(*All this very excited.*)

DAVID.   I shall be very pleased.   (*Looking at her.*)

DUL.   You're thinking about me.

DAVID.   I was thinking that a mother is the most beautiful thing on earth.

DUL.   Oh, you don't know!   You can't imagine! She's over two years old, and I haven't got over remembering that she's mine.   Every time I think of her I feel a little catch here in the very middle of my heart, a delicious little stab, as if some angel came behind me and whispered to me, "God has made you a present of ten hundred thousand million pounds all your own."   Oh, she makes up to me for everything.

(DAVID *is approaching her with great tenderness*

when HELEN *enters with* ROSY, *the two-years-old baby, in her arms in nightclothes.*)

DUL. (*rushes to* HELEN). There! There! You may look at her!

HELEN. Hush! She's asleep!

DUL. I must kiss her if it kills her! (*Hugging the baby, kisses her, lifts the nightgown, kisses the baby's feet, croons over it—points her finger mockingly at* REMON *in childlike mockery and laughter.*) There! There! There, Mr. Philosopher from Andromeda! You can't say a mother's love isn't real!

DAVID. I never did. It's the one thing that shows what a sham the rest of the world is. That little star in Andromeda is crowded with mothers. They've all been there once in their lives.

(*Bends over the baby for a moment.*)

DUL. (*excited, feverish*). Nell, Mr. Remon has an odd notion that this world isn't real.

HELEN. The cure for that is to earn half-a-crown a day and live on it.

DAVID. Oh yes, I know. Work is real.

(*Bends over the baby.*)

DUL. (*to* DAVID). What are you looking at? (*Scrutinises him carefully; then suddenly, with savage earnestness, half despair, half entreaty.*) She's like *me?* She's like *me!!* (*crescendo, tigerish, frenzied*). Say she's like *me!!!*

DAVID (*very quietly*). She is like *you.* (*Kisses the child reverently.*) She is wholly like *you!*

DUL. (*stands absorbed, very quietly*). Take her back again to the nursery, Nell.

(*Stands troubled, absorbed.*)

HELEN. Good-night, Mr. Remon.

DAVID. Good-night.

(*Goes towards the door with her.*)

HELEN (*to* DAVID, *smiling*). I've just remembered something else that is real.

DAVID. What's that?

HELEN. Duty.

(*Exit with baby. A summer sunrise shines pink through the conservatory, and lights up the room with summer morning light.* DAVID *returns to* DULCIE, *who stands absorbed.*)

DAVID. Lady Skene, I asked to see you because —it is necessary for me to leave England very soon.

DUL. No—no!

DAVID. Yes—yes. I never use the word "honour" about my conduct, because every scamp has used it until it's the most counterfeit word in the language. But I've just learned that if I stay in England I shall injure very deeply a friend of mine, so naturally I'm going away.

DUL. But—tell me—(*pause*)—what——

DAVID. If I stay I cannot continue an honest man. Will you let it rest there?

DUL. If you wish——

DAVID (*after a little pause, with some embarrassment*). I have just heard—I scarcely know how to mention it—that you may be placed in a position of some difficulty.

DUL. You mean that Sir Brice is ruined. In one way it's a relief, because at any rate it will break up this life, and I'm so tired of it.

DAVID. Yet you thought you would like it on that night of the Hunt Ball.

DUL. Yes. I longed for it. Is life like that all through?

DAVID. Like what?

DUL. To long for a thing very much and to find it worthless, and then to long for something else much more—to be sure that this is worth having—to get it, and then to find that that is worthless too. And so on, and so on, and so on?

DAVID. I'm afraid life is very much like that on this particular planet.

DUL. Oh, but that would be awful if I found out that——(*stops*).

DAVID. What?

DUL. Nothing. You remember that night of the Hunt Ball?

DAVID (*nods*). It was the last time I saw my friend George Copeland. He died in Alaska six months after.

DUL. And you went away for over a year.

DAVID. No—only for a few weeks. After Copeland's funeral I went to the Mediterranean to choose a site for my observatory, and I was back in England within less than three months.

DUL. But we never saw you till last season. Where were you?

DAVID. When you were in the country, I was there; when you were in town I was in town too. I have never been far away from you. I have kept an account of every time I have seen you for the last three years.

DUL. (*looks at him as if suddenly struck with a thought*). Tell me—where were you two years ago last March?

DAVID. At Gerard's Heath—near you.

DUL. (*suddenly*). Did you—the night Rosy was—I mean the night of the second—it was a dreadful snowstorm——

DAVID. I remember.

DUL. One of my nurses said she saw some one in the garden. (*Looks at him.*)

DAVID. It was I. Your life was in danger. I passed those two nights outside your window.

(DULCIE, *with great affection, involuntarily puts her hand on his arm.*)

HELEN *re-enters.*

HELEN. Sir Brice has just come back and is in the smoking-room downstairs.

DUL. (*turning*). Look! It's morning.

DAVID. Good-bye.

DUL. (*suddenly*). No—I must have another word with you. Wait here a moment. (*Goes to archway and looks off; comes back.*) Here is Sir Brice. Nell, take Mr. Remon on to the balcony for a minute or two and wait there with him till Sir Brice has gone upstairs.

(*Exeunt* DAVID *and* HELEN *through conservatory and on to balcony.*)

SIR BRICE *enters, looking a little flushed and dissipated.*

SIR BRICE (*staring at* DULCIE; *after a pause*). Well?

DUL. Well?

SIR BRICE (*drops into a chair; whistles*). Got rid of your friends?

DUL. All except Mr. Remon. He's on the balcony with Nell.

SIR BRICE. Oh! (*Pause. Whistles; takes some change out of his pocket—three shillings and threepence; places the coins very carefully and elaborately in a longitudinal position on the palm of his left hand, arranging the three shillings and the three pennies in a line, whistling carelessly.*) That's our net fortune, my girl. (*Holding them up under her face.*) That is our precise capital —three shillings and threepence. (*Whistles.*) Not another farthing. And some thousand pounds' worth of debts.

DUL. (*unconcerned*). Indeed.

SIR BRICE (*with a sudden little burst of brutality—not too marked*). Look here! can't you get some money?

DUL. What do you mean?

SIR BRICE. *Get some money!* That's plain English, isn't it?

DUL. I don't understand you.

SIR BRICE. This fellow Remon is devilish fond of you. Can't you get some money from him?

DUL. Hush! Borrow money from him!

SIR BRICE (*suggestively*). You needn't borrow. (DULCIE *looks at him inquiringly.*) Now can't you get some?

> (DULCIE *looks at him for a moment; she raises her fan to strike him; sees* DAVID, *who has entered from conservatory.* HELEN *stands at conservatory door.*)

DAVID. Lady Skene, I have been obliged to overhear what has just been said. To-morrow morning I leave for the South of France, and I shall be quite inaccessible for some years. My bankers will have orders to send you a cheque-book and to honour your signature to any extent that you are likely to require. (DULCIE *makes a protest.*) If you please— if you please. As I shall be away from England there cannot be the least slur upon you in accepting it. Miss Larondie, you will be with your sister, always. She will be in your care—always. (*Shakes hands with* HELEN.) Be very kind to her. Never leave her. Good-bye.

DUL.   But I—cannot—take——

DAVID (*silencing her*). If you please—It is my last request. Good-bye.

>   (SIR BRICE, *who has been sitting all the while, listening, rises.)* ·

DAVID (*looks at him for just half a moment ; looks at* DULCIE). Good-bye.   (*Exit.*)

(*Nine months pass between Acts II. and III.*)

ACT III

*A rather handsome modern room furnished in French
hotel fashion. Two long windows, right, curtained.
Door at back. Door left. Small card table down
stage, left, with several packs of cards loosely on it.
The whole floor round the table strewn with cards.
A cloak of DULCIE'S on chair at back. Discover
SIR BRICE in evening dress seated left of table, aim-
lessly and mechanically playing with the cards.
After a few seconds DULCIE, in dinner dress, enters
from door at back, crosses to the window and stands
looking out, having taken no notice of SIR BRICE.
As she enters he leaves off playing with the cards for
a moment, looks at her.*

SIR BRICE (*in rather a commanding tone, a little
brutal*). Come here.

(DULCIE *takes no notice. A little pause.*)

SIR BRICE (*louder*).   D'ye hear?   Come h
        (DULCIE *comes down to him, does not ....*
             He looks up at her.   Her face is quite
             blank, looking indifferently in front of her.)

SIR BRICE (*begins playing with cards again*).   I've lost over six hundred pounds.   (DULCIE *takes no notice.*)

SIR BRICE (*dashes the pack of cards under his feet, stamps on them*).   Damn and *damn* the cards!
        (DULCIE *takes no notice.   Slight pause.*)

SIR BRICE (*roars out*).   The hotel people have sent up their bill again with a request for payment.
        (*Slight pause.*   DULCIE *goes back to the*
             window, stands there looking out.   Pause.)

SIR BRICE (*roars out furiously*).   Why the devil don't you get something for that deafness of yours! (*Suddenly jumps up, goes up to her, seizes her hands, turns her round.*)   Now look here——

Hotel Servant *enters, left, with letter on tray.*   SIR
    BRICE *desists.   The* Hotel Servant *brings the letter*
    to DULCIE, *who crosses and takes it.   Exit*
    Servant.   DULCIE *opens letter, reads it.*

SIR BRICE.   Well?   (DULCIE *rings bell.*)
SIR BRICE.   Well?

Servant *enters.*

DUL. (*in cold equable tone, to* SIR BRICE).   Mr. Edward Remon wishes to see me.   He asks me to

excuse his being in fancy dress. He's going to the
Opera Ball. Shall I see him here or in the hall?

SIR BRICE. Here.

DUL. (*to* Servant). Show Mr. Remon here.

(*Exit* Servant.)

SIR BRICE (*to* DULCIE). Where's his brother, the
astronomer?

DUL. At his observatory, I suppose. I've not
seen him since the night we began to live upon him.

Hotel Servant *enters, announces* MR. EDWARD REMON.
*EDDIE enters, dressed as Pierrot for the fancy dress
ball. Exit* Servant.

EDDIE (*all through the Act very excited*). How d'ye
do? (*To* DULCIE; *shakes hands with her. To* SIR
BRICE.) How d'ye do?

SIR BRICE. How d'ye do?

(*Looks meaningly at* DULCIE *and exit left.*)

EDDIE. So good of you to excuse this dress.

DUL. Your brother?

EDDIE. He's down in the town with me to-night.
We've been dining at the Café de Paris. I've taken
three glasses of champagne—anything more than a
spoonful makes me tipsy, and so, with that and this
dress, and our journey to Africa, I'm quite mad to-night.

DUL. Africa!

EDDIE. We start early to-morrow morning to
the deadliest place on the West Coast.

DUL.   Not your brother?

EDDIE.   Yes.   We're going to watch the transit
of Venus, and as there was a jolly lot of fever there
all the other astronomers rather funked it.   So Davy
has fitted out an expedition himself.   (DULCIE *shows
great concern.*   EDDIE *rattles on.*)   I'm going to have
a spree to-night.   I've never been drunk in my life,
and I thought I should like to try what it's like—
because—(*tossing up a coin*) it's heads we come back
alive and prove Davy's theory about sun-spots—and
it's tails we leave our bones and all our apparatus
out there.   It's tails—we're as dead as door-nails.
(*Sees* DULCIE'S *pained face.*)   Lady Skene—I'm so
sorry——

DUL.   We've been three weeks in Nice.   Why
hasn't your brother come to see me?

EDDIE.   A mistaken sense of duty.   Davy has the
oddest notions about duty.   He thinks one ought to
do it when it's unpleasant.   So do I when I'm in my
right clothes, and my right senses, but now I'm half
tipsy, and have got a fool's cap on, I can see quite
plainly that duty's all moonshine.   Duty is doing
exactly what one likes, and it's Davy's duty to come
to you.   And the fool is just breaking his heart for a
sight of you.   Shall I find him and bring him?

DUL.   Where is he?

EDDIE.   He's in the town getting everything
ready for to-morrow.   Shall I find him?

DUL. (*looking at her watch*).   Quarter to eleven.   I

may be alone in half an hour.   Yes, bring him to me
here.

EDDIE.   Hurrah !—*Au revoir.*

> (*Exit left.   Short pause.*   SIR BRICE *appears
> at the same door, looks after* EDDIE,
> *shuts door, enters.*)

SIR BRICE (*to* DULCIE).   Well ?

> (DULCIE *does not reply, goes to her room at
> back,* SIR BRICE *follows her, the door is
> closed in his face and a lock is heard to
> turn.*   SIR BRICE *shakes the door handle,
> kicks the door, looks vicious and spiteful,
> comes down a step or two, kicks a hassock.*)

Servant *enters, announcing* MR. LUSHINGTON.   *Enter*
MONTY.   SIR BRICE *nods.*

MON.   Well, dear chum !   (*Looking round at the
cards on the floor.*)   Did you give Fancourt his
revenge ?

SIR BRICE (*kicking cards on the floor*).   Damn the
cards.

MON.   By all means.   How's Lady Skene ?

SIR BRICE (*kicking cards, mutters*).   —mn Lady Skene.

MON.   By all means.

SIR BRICE.   You're married, Lushington——

MON.   I am three months a bridegroom.

SIR BRICE.   Why the devil did you get married ?

MON.   Because I ascertained that my wife would
have seven thousand a year.   Why did you ?

SIR BRICE.   Because I was a silly fool.

MON.   Well, there couldn't be two better reasons for getting married. .

SIR BRICE (*furious with his cards*). —mn everything and everybody.

MON.   By all means. And now we've reached finality and are utterly the sport of destiny, will you do me a good turn?

SIR BRICE.   What?

MON.   I'm going to take a lady to the Opera Ball, and I fear Lady Clarice will be dull, or I should say *restless*, in my absence. I know you will be going to the Cercle d'Amérique to wreck your farthing chance of eternity at poker.

SIR BRICE.   Well?

MON.   It would momentarily reinstate your celestial hopes if you would tell Lady Skene that I'm going to the club with you, and persuade her to spend the lonely hours of her widowhood with Lady Clarice in number one-four-three. They will doubtless tear our characters to rags, but that will keep them from the worse mischief of interfering with us.

SIR BRICE.   Will you do me a good turn?

MON.   Anything in my power.

SIR BRICE.   Lend me a couple of hundred pounds.

MON.   My dear Bricey! If my I.O.U., or my name, or my presence, is good for anything at the Cercle d'Amérique, you're welcome to it.

SIR BRICE. Will you come with me and set me afloat for a quarter of an hour?

MON. Certainly.

SIR BRICE. I'll ask Lady Skene. (*Goes up to the door at back, raps.*) Are you there? (*A little louder.*) Are you there?

MON. Throw in a "my dear," Bricey, or some such trifle. Its effect will be in proportion to its scarcity.

SIR BRICE. My dear (*rapping still*). Mr. Lushington has called. (*Rapping.*) Do you hear, my love? (*With a grim sneer on the last word. The door is a little opened.* SIR BRICE *forces his way in.*) Lady Clarice wants to know if you will go and sit with her while——

(*The remainder of sentence is lost by the closing of door after him.*)

LADY CLARICE *enters door, left, with opera cloak.*

MON. (*showing surprise, which he instantly checks*). Where so gay and free, my love?

CLAR. (*looking him straight in the face very determinedly*). To the Opera Ball.

MON. Oh.

CLAR. You're going to take that woman.

MON. I know many *ladies*, but no *women*.

Door, left, opens.   Servant *enters.*

CHAR. (*her voice heard outside*). Yes. See if Mr. Lushington is there, and say a lady is waiting for him in the hall.

G

SERV. A lady is waiting for you, sir.

(MONTY *is going.* LADY CLARICE *makes a little movement to intercept him.*)

MON. (*in a low voice*). Don't be foolish.

(*Exit* Servant.)

CHAR. (*her voice at door, outside*). Aren't you nearly ready, Monty? (*Appears at door, sees* LADY CLARICE, *takes in the situation at a glance, has a slight shock, but instantly recovers herself. Runs to* LADY CLARICE *brimming with affection.*) *Darling*, are you going too? So pleased! So charmed! How sweet of you!   (*Offers to kiss* LADY CLARICE.)

CLAR. (*indignantly*). How dare you!

MON. (*stepping between them*). Hush! (*To* CLARICE.) What's the use of having a row here, or anywhere? For Heaven's sake, do be a good sensible girl, and don't shatter the happiness of our married life before—before we know where we are. Charley and I are going to the Opera Ball, will you come with us?

CLAR. (*indignant*). What!

MON. Or go by yourself. Or go with any one you please. Or go anywhere or do anything in the world you like. Only don't make a scene here.

CLAR. My father shall know.

MON. Very well. Very well. We'll discuss that by and by. But do recognise once and for all the futility of rows. You'd better come with us.

CLAR. Come with you?

CHAR. (*begins*). My dear Clarice, I assure you——

MON. (*stops* CHARLEY *with a warning look*). For Heaven's sake, Clarice, whatever we do, do not let us make ourselves ridiculous. (*Re-enter* SIR BRICE. MONTY *snatches up* LADY CLARICE'S *arm. She reluctantly allows him to do so.*) All right, Bricey. Sorry I can't come with you to the club—but I've persuaded Lady Clarice and Lady Shalford to come to the Opera Ball with me. Bye, bye, dear crony, our love to Lady Skene. Hope you will have as pleasant an evening as we shall—Ta! Ta!

> (*Exit with great animation*, LADY CLARICE
> *holding reluctantly and aloof on one arm*,
> CHARLEY *more affectionate on the other.*
> *As soon as he has gone* SIR BRICE *goes
> to* DULCIE'S *door, throws it wide open,
> stands back, calls.*)

SIR BRICE. Now, will you let us understand each other once for all?

DULCIE *enters, looks at him without speaking.*

SIR BRICE. I want some money. This fellow Remon has offered you his purse to any extent. Get a few hundreds for me to go on with.

DUL. No.

SIR BRICE. You won't? Then why did you begin to take his money?

Dul. Because I was weak, because you bullied me, and because I knew I was welcome.

Sir Brice. Very good. The same reasons continue. You're weak, I'm a bully, and you're welcome. (*Coming to her.*) Aren't you welcome, eh? Aren't you welcome?·

Dul. I believe I am welcome to every penny he has in the world.

Sir Brice. He loves you?

Dul. Yes.

Sir Brice. And you love him?

Dul. (*looking straight at* Sir Brice *very fearlessly and calmly*). With all my heart.

Sir Brice. And you aren't ashamed to tell me?

Dul. Is there anything in your past life that you have taken the trouble to hide from me? Have you ever openly or secretly had an attachment to any living creature that does you as much credit and so little shame as my love for David Remon does to me?

Sir Brice. All right (*whistles*). Go on loving him. You needn't hesitate. He expects a fair exchange—if he hasn't already got it.

Dul. (*very calmly*). That's a lie, and you know it is.

Sir Brice. Very well. It's a lie. I don't care one way or the other. Get me some money.

Dul. You have had the last farthing that you will ever touch of David Remon's money.

Sir Brice. All right. (*Whistles, jumps up very*

determinedly.) Then you've seen the last you will see
of your child for some years to come.

DUL. (*aroused*). What ! you will hit me through
my child !

SIR BRICE. I think *my* child's health requires a
change for a few years—a different climate from you
and myself. We will go upon a little tour by ourselves, shall we ? to—where the devil shall we go ?
I don't care. I shall send Rosy away to-morrow
morning. D'ye hear.

DUL. I hear.

SIR BRICE. If I don't see you again to-night, get
her ready by to-morrow morning.   (*Exit.*)

DUL. (*stands for a moment or two quiet, then bursts
into a fit of ironic laughter*). Nell ! (*Goes to the
door at back, calls out.*) Nell ! Nell ! Come here !

HELEN *enters.*

HELEN. What's the matter ?

DUL. Nell, old girl, have you got such a thing as
a Church Service about you ?

HELEN. Church Service ?

DUL. I want you to tell me the end and meaning
of marriage. There's something about it in the
Church Service, isn't there ? I did go through it
once, I know, but I've forgotten what it's all about.
What does it mean ?

HELEN. Marriage ?

DUL. Yes. Oh, I know! (*Clapping her hands childishly.*) It's one of Mr. Remon's games.

HELEN. Games?

DUL. Yes. He says men and women are playing a lot of queer games on earth that they call religion, love, politics, and this and that and the other— marriage must be one, and it's the funniest of them all! It's a two-handed game like—like cribbage, or tossing up. You choose your partner—head's he's a good 'un, then you're in clover; tails he's a bad 'un, then it's purgatory and inferno for you for the rest of your life, unless you're a man. It's all right if you're a man. The same game as before, choose your partner—heads she's a good 'un, then you're in clover; tails she's a bad 'un, then you cut her, and toss up again and again, until you do get a good 'un. That's the game—that's the game—and it's a splendid game for a man.

(*Throwing herself in low armchair.*)

Servant *enters, announces* MR. BLANCHFLOWER. BLANCHFLOWER, *in evening dress, pops in.*

BLAN. How d'ye do, Lady Skene? Am I in the way, eh? (*Exit* Servant.)

DUL. (*is leaning back, her head on the back of the armchair, looking up to the ceiling, her hands on its arms*). Enter! Enter! Enter! You're just in time. Help us solve this mighty question.

BLAN. Something important, eh?

DUL. No, only marriage.

BLAN. What about it?

DUL. Well — what about it? Give us your opinion. There's something mystical about it, isn't there? Nell, where's that Church Service? Something mystical?

BLAN. Well, yes; and—hum? eh? (*happy thought*) —something ideal——

DUL. Mystical and ideal. Go on, Nell.

HELEN. I'd rather not. I don't like to hear you mocking at marriage.

DUL. (*laughing*). Mocking at marriage! Oh, my God! is it women who have married bad men that mock at marriage! Make haste, make haste! (*Dashing her hands on the chair.*) Marriage is a mystical, ideal state—isn't there something in the Service about physical? Go on, Nell, go on—help us out. Go on! What have we left out?

HELEN. The wife's duty.

DUL. Yah. Yah. Yah.

> (*This is very quiet and calm, with a pause between each Yah, very different from the excited Yah! Yah! Yah! of the second Act.*)

HELEN. To her husband to keep her vows. To herself to keep herself pure and stainless, because it is her glory, as it is a man's glory to be brave and honest.

DUL. (*same position, same tone*). Yah. Yah. Yah.

HELEN. And to society, to her nation, because no nation has ever survived whose women have been immoral.

DUL. (*suddenly springing up, sitting up upright in the chair*). And the men?

HELEN. I don't know whether it's a man's duty to be moral. I'm sure it's a woman's.

DUL. Oh, then marriage is a moral state, eh—at least for women, eh, Mr. Blanchflower?

BLAN. (*who has shown symptoms of great discomfort through the interview*). Ye—es—decidedly marriage is—or—a—should be a moral state.

DUL. (*jumping up vigorously*). Ah, now we've got it! Now we can go ahead! Marriage is a physical, mystical, ideal, moral game. Oh, I hate these words, moral, ideal. How if it isn't ideal? Suppose it's horribly, horribly real! How if it isn't moral? Suppose it's horribly, horribly immoral! Moral! Moral!! Moral!!! Is there anything under God's sun so immoral, ah—guess it—guess it—to be married to a man one hates! And you go on plastering it and poulticing it and sugaring it over with "moral" and "ideal" and "respectable," and all those words that men use to cheat themselves with. It isn't moral to be married to a man one hates! It isn't ideal! It isn't mystical! It's hateful! It's martyrdom! (*A long pause.*)

BLAN. (*calm, with a real touch of feeling*). My

dear Lady Skene, I won't pretend to offer you advice——

DUL. (*has recovered from her outburst, now speaks in a very calm, indifferent, matter-of-fact tone*). It doesn't matter. You're going to the ball?

BLAN. I was going—but if I can help you in any way——(*Struck with the idea.*) My uncle, Canon Butterfield, is here for the winter. He suffers from liver, and has written a book on Socinianism. If you want any spiritual advice, I'm sure you couldn't do better.

DUL. What is Socinianism? Is it anything to do with marriage?

BLAN. Well—ah—no. Shall I send him?

DUL. No, I won't trouble you. I'll think this out for myself.

BLAN. Well, if you ever do need a clergyman, don't forget my uncle. You can't do better. Or if at any time I can be of any use——

DUL. Thank you. Good-night.

BLAN. (*shaking hands very sympathetically*). Good-bye.   (*Exit.*)

DUL. (*suddenly*). Nell! (HELEN *comes to her.*) Take Rosy up at once, dress her, get out of the hotel by the servants' way so that you don't meet Sir Brice —take her over to Beaulieu to the Hôtel des Anglais, and wait there till to-morrow morning. I'll send you a message what to do.

Servant *enters, announces* Mr. Remon—Mr. Edward
   Remon.   *Enter* David *and* Eddie, *still in Pierrot's
   dress.*   Helen *shows some surprise.*

(*Exit* Servant.)

Dul.   Quick, Nell, do as I tell you.

Helen (*looking at* David *and* Eddie).   Promise
me——

Dul.   What?

Helen.   You'll take no step till you've seen me.

Dul.   I promise.   Make haste.   Come here and
tell me when Rosy's ready.

Helen (*comes to* David, *shakes hands with him*).
You heard her promise.

David.   She shall keep it.   (*Exit* Helen *at back.*)

Eddie.   I've brought him, Lady Skene.   I'm off
to the ball.   I'm not so tipsy now as I was, but I'm
going to have my fling.   It's my only chance of
going to the devil.   Davy, where shall I meet you?

David.   I'll come to the Opera House for you.
Wait for me there.

Eddie.   Come as soon as you can, won't you?
You come too, Lady Skene.   You can't think how
jolly it is to have no duty and no conscience and no
faith and no future, no anything but pleasure and
life!   Do come!   Let's all be fools for once in our
lives!   Let's be monkeys again!   Come on!   Come
on!

(*Exit.   As soon as he has gone,* David *and*

DULCIE, *who have been standing on opposite sides of the room, go to each other very calmly. They meet in the middle of the room, take each other's hands. He raises hers to his lips. DAVID'S appearance has changed since the last Act; he is more worn and spiritual, a little greyer, very calm at first, an unearthly look in his face. They stand looking at each other for some moments.*)

DUL. You're changed! You're not well!

DAVID. Quite well. So well, I feel no ill can ever happen to me.

DUL. Why did you not come to me before?

DAVID. I'd been able to do you a service. I didn't wish you to think that I had any claim on you.

DUL. Ah, you shouldn't misunderstand me. I could never misunderstand you like that. I've taken your money. I knew I was welcome, because —if I were rich and you were poor, I would give you all I had.

DAVID. Ah! Take all I have!

DUL. Not another farthing.

DAVID. Why not?

DUL. I would be proud to owe all my happiness, all my comfort to you. I have been proud these last six months to think that my child's very bread came from you.

DAVID.   Ah!   (*Coming nearer to her.*)

DUL.   I would only have taken just sufficient for necessaries—but he forced me.   I was weak.   Now the end has come.   I won't waste any more of your money in this (*pointing to the cards*) and racing, and —I don't know what.

DAVID.   Tell me all.

DUL.   Things can't go on as they are.   (*Smiling.*) Do you remember the Scotchman who lost his mother-in-law and his aunt and three cousins, all in one epidemic?   He said it was "just reedeeclous." Things are "just reedeeclous" with me.   (*Laughing.*) Sir Brice has threatened to take Rosy away from me.

DAVID.   No!

DUL.   Yes!   I'm sending Nell to Beaulieu with her to-night.   I don't know what will happen.   I don't think I care much.   It doesn't matter.   Nothing matters.   (*Smiling.   Then with sudden alarm.*)   Yes— this journey of yours to Africa.   Must you go?

DAVID.   I must.   I've been waiting for years for this chance.   If I succeed, it will crown all my life's work.

DUL.   But it's dangerous.

DAVID.   I take a doctor and drugs.   Besides, I bear a charmed life.

DUL.   But this fever,—Eddie says it is deadly.

DAVID (*with great calmness, looking away*).   It will pass me.   But if it kills me I must go.

DUL.   No, no, no.

DAVID. Yes, yes, yes. I'm pledged. All my world, the little world that takes an interest in me, is watching me. There's the hope of a great prize. It's my one chance of snatching the poor little laurel-wreath that we mortals call immortality.

DUL. But can't you go some other time?

DAVID. I must be at my post, especially as it is a little dangerous,—that makes it the post of honour. I've delayed everything till the last moment that I might be near you till the very end.

DUL. The end! Then this is the end? I shall never see you again.

DAVID. Yes. When I return.

DUL. (*shaking her head*). You will not return. (*Looking at him very keenly and closely.*) Tell me, in your heart of hearts do you not know that you will never come back?

DAVID (*is about to speak*).

DUL. Ah no—tell me the truth!

DAVID (*slowly and fatefully*). I wonder how it is that when one has carefully weeded out all the old superstitions from one's mind, a crop of new superstitions springs up more foolish than the old ones. I've lived up there so long I've grown morbid. I've an attack of the silliest form of superstition—a presentiment.

DUL. Ah, I knew it!

DAVID. In six months I shall laugh at it. We will laugh at it together.

DUL. (*determinedly*). You shall not go!

DAVID. I must. I'm working with my comrades all over the world. I've undertaken this part of the work. If I don't carry it out I break faith with them and spoil their work too. All the good fellows who are going with me and sharing in my dangers are waiting for me at Marseilles. I can't leave them in the lurch—I can't—you would not have me do it! Say you wouldn't have me stamp myself a coward, a deserter.

DUL. No, no. But I don't want you to go. (*Approaching him.*) If I asked you to stay——

DAVID. You will not—(*Going towards her.*) You will not (*a little nearer*) ask me to stay. (*She looks at him—gradually they go closer to each other, and his manner changes from a calm, dreamy, fateful tone to a fierce, hoarse, passionate tone.*) Do you know what it means if I stay? Dulcie!

DUL. You never called me that before.

DAVID (*clasping her*). I've never been so near to you. Dulcie! (*With sudden, mad abandonment, clasping her passionately.*) Yes, I'll stay! I'll stay! Tell me to stay because—because—you love me.

DUL. Stay—because—ah, you know I love you!

DAVID. Eddie's right. Let's be fools to-night! Let's live to-night! I'm hungry for you! Dulcie, tell me once again that you love me.

DUL. No—no. Forget it. What have I said? What shall we do?

DAVID. I don't know. What does it matter? We will go to this ball—anything—anywhere! Our lives are in our own hands. Come with me.

(*Leading her towards door, left.*)

SIR BRICE *enters. He shuts the door, stands against it, his feet a little sprawling, his hands in his pockets, looking at them maliciously. Long pause.* HELEN *enters at the other door. Another pause. She beckons* DULCIE.

HELEN. Dulcie! (*Indicates the inside room.* DULCIE *goes up to her.*)

(*Exit* HELEN. DULCIE *at the door looks at the two men. Exit* DULCIE. *The two men are left alone. Another slight pause.* SIR BRICE *walks very deliberately up to* DAVID. *The two men stand close to each other for a moment or two.*)

SIR BRICE. You've come to settle your little account, I suppose?

DAVID. I owe you nothing.

SIR BRICE. But I owe you six thousand pounds. I haven't a penny in the world. I'll cut you for it, double or quits.

DAVID. I don't play cards.

SIR BRICE. You'd better begin.

(*Rapping on the table with the cards.*)

DAVID (*very firmly*). I don't play cards with *you*.

SIR BRICE.   And I say you shall.

DAVID (*very stern and contemptuous*).   I don't play cards with you.

> (*Going towards door;* SIR BRICE *following him up.*)

SIR BRICE.   You refuse?

DAVID.   I refuse.

SIR BRICE (*stopping him*).   Once for all, will you give me a chance of paying back the six thousand pounds that Lady Skene has borrowed from you? Yes or no?

DAVID.   No.

SIR BRICE.   No?

DAVID (*very emphatically*).   No.   (*Goes to door, suddenly turns round, comes up to him.*)   Yes.   (*Comes to the table.*)   I *do* play cards with you.   You want my money.   Very well.   I'll give you a chance of winning all I have in the world.

SIR BRICE (*after a look of astonishment*).   Good. I'm your man.   Any game you like, and any stakes.

DAVID (*very calm, cold, intense tone all through*). The stakes on my side are some two hundred thousand pounds.   The stakes on your side are—your wife and child.

SIR BRICE (*taken aback*).   My wife and child!

DAVID.   Your wife and child.   Come—begin! (*Points to the cards.*)

SIR BRICE (*getting flurried*).   My wife and child? (*Puts his hands restlessly through his hair, looks intently*

at DAVID. *Pause.*) All right. (*Pause. Cunningly.*)
I value my wife and child very highly.

DAVID. I value them at all I have in the world.
(*Pointing to cards.*) Begin!

SIR BRICE. You seem in a hurry.

DAVID. I believe I haven't six months to live. I
want to make the most of those six months. If I
have more I want to make the most of all the years.
Begin!

SIR BRICE (*wipes his face with his handkerchief*).
This is the first time I've played this game. We'd
better arrange conditions.

DAVID. There's only one condition. We play
till I'm beggared of every farthing I have, or till
you're beggared of them. Sit down!

SIR BRICE (*sits down*). Very well. (*Pause.*) What
game?

DAVID. The shortest.

SIR BRICE. Simple cutting?

DAVID. What you please. Begin!

SIR BRICE. There's no hurry. I mean to have a
night's fun out of this.

DAVID. Look at me. Don't trifle with me! I
want to have done with you. I want them to have
done with you. I want to get them away from you.
Quick! I want to know now—now—this very
moment—whether they are yours or mine. Begin.

SIR BRICE (*shuffles the cards*). All right. What
do we cut for?

DAVID. Let one cut settle it.

SIR BRICE. No. It's too much to risk on one throw.

DAVID. One cut. Begin.

SIR BRICE. It's too big. I can't. (*Gets up; walks about a pace or two.*) I like high play, but that's too high for me. (DAVID *remains at back of table, very calm; does not stir all through the scene;* SIR BRICE *walking about.*) No, by Jove! I'll tell you what I'll do. Three cuts out of five. Damn it all! I'm game! Two out of three. By Jove, two out of three! Will that do?

DAVID. So be it! Shuffle. Sit down!

> (SIR BRICE *sits down; begins shuffling the cards. All through the scene he is nervous, excited, hysterical, laughing.* DAVID *as cold as a statue.*)

SIR BRICE (*having shuffled*). Now then. Who cuts first?

DULCIE *enters at back.*

DUL. (*surprised*). Mr. Remon! No! No! Not that! Not that!

DAVID (*coming down, warning her off with a motion of his hand*). If you please. Stand aside for a moment. (*Offers the cards to* SIR BRICE *to cut.*)

SIR BRICE. Ace counts lowest.

DAVID. As you will. Cut. (SIR BRICE *cuts.*)

SIR BRICE. King! By Jove! King! Cut!

> (DAVID *cuts.*)

SIR BRICE. Nine! One to me! By Jove! one to me! (*To* DULCIE.) Give us up some of those cards, will you?

> (DAVID *by a gesture stops her; takes up the cards and shuffles them.*)

SIR BRICE. Shuffle up! By Jove! if I win——

DUL. Mr. Remon, you'll not play any more?

DAVID (*very gently*). Stand aside, please.

SIR BRICE. No. Let her shuffle for us. She's in it, isn't she?

DUL. What do you mean? What are you playing for?

SIR BRICE. You'd like to know, would you? What are we playing for? I'll tell you. We're playing for you and your child!

DUL. (*suddenly*). What? (*Shows great horror and astonishment.*) Mr. Remon! It's not so? It's not so? (*To* DAVID.) What are you playing for?

DAVID. He has said. For you and your child. If I win, will you abide by the bargain? (*Very long pause—she looks from one to the other.*)

DUL. Yes.

DAVID (*same calm tone—to* SIR BRICE). Shuffle.

> (*They both shuffle cards.*)

SIR BRICE (*very excited, laughing, nervous*). You've got to win both now. You know that?

DAVID. I know.

> (*Holds the cards he has shuffled to* SIR BRICE.)

SIR BRICE (*cuts*). Ten. Not bad. You've got to beat it. Cut!

(*Holds the cards he has shuffled to* DAVID. DAVID *cuts.*)

SIR BRICE. Queen! One each! Now for the final, d'ye hear? This is final. If I win——(*Walking about excitedly; pours out a glass of brandy— drinks.*) I'll cut first! No! damn it all! you cut first! (*Holding cards.* DAVID *cuts.*) Eight! (*To* DAVID, *suddenly.*) Suppose I win—you'll pay me? You mean to pay me?

DAVID. I shall pay you every farthing.

SIR BRICE. What security do you give me?

DAVID. My word in the presence of the woman I love.

SIR BRICE (*walks about*). Let me be a moment. (*Walks about; takes up brandy; drinks a glass.*)

DAVID. Cut.

SIR BRICE (*to* DULCIE). You're anxious, are you? I'm going to win! I mean it! I'm going to win! (*To* DAVID.) Now! (DAVID *holds cards;* SIR BRICE *cuts.*) My God! I've lost!

DAVID (*throws down the card-table; leaps at him; catches hold of him by the throat*). Yes, you've lost! She's mine! (*Gets him down on his knees.*) You've cheated me of her all these years! You've cheated me of her love, cheated me of the fatherhood of her child, you've dragged her down, you've dishonoured her! She's my wife now—my wife and child! Take

your oath you'll never lay claim to them again!
Swear it!   (*Shaking him.*)

SIR BRICE. She's yours! Take her! I'll never
see her or her child again! I swear it! Take them!

DAVID. Dare to break your word—dare to lay a
finger on her or her child—dare to show your face in
the home that my love shall give to her—and whatever laws men have made to bind you and her
together, I'll break them and rid her of you! D'ye
hear? She's mine! She's mine! She's mine!
(*Throws* SIR BRICE *back on the floor. To* DULCIE.)
My wife! My child! Come! You're mine!
(DULCIE *takes up her cloak, which has been lying on
chair at back.*)   (*Exeunt* DAVID *and* DULCIE.)

ACT IV

SCENE—THE OBSERVATORY ON MONT GARIDELLI IN THE MARITIME ALPS, NEAR NICE

A door, right. A large fireplace, with pine cones and pine logs ready laid, above door, right. At the back, seen through a large curtained doorway, is the circular Observatory with large telescope. This room is vaguely seen, the telescope being lighted by a shaft of moonlight at the beginning of the Act. On the left side, slant-wise, a large window, with terrace outside, giving scenery of the Maritime Alps. A large armchair above the fireplace. On table and scattered about the room are a number of scientific books and astronomical instruments and apparatus. The window is curtained with Eastern curtains. As curtain rises the whole scene is dark except for the shaft of moonlight that falls on the telescope.

Enter DAVID *with lamp in one hand, leading* DULCIE *with the other.*

DAVID. Come in! Come to your home! My wife!

DUL. (*cold, shuddering*). Ah no—don't call me that—at least not yet.

DAVID. You're shivering! Let me give you some wine.

> (*Goes to cupboard, brings out bottle and glass, places them on table.*)

DUL. No, no, tell me——(*Goes to him, looks into his face.*)

DAVID (*with great tenderness*). Dulcie! Dulcie! What is it, dear? How cold you are. I'll light the fire. (*Lights fire, which is already laid with large pine cones and logs and quickly blazes up.*) I'm your servant now. I've nothing to do all my life but wait on you. We shall soon have a blaze with these pine logs. My servants left me last night. I thought I should have no further use for them. I thought my life here was ended. Ended! My life has only begun this last hour. (*Clasping her.*) Dulcie! Do you know where you are? You are in your home. Take off your hat and cloak, dear. (*Gently removes her hat and cloak.*) There! (*Seats her at the fire in large chair.*) This is your own hearth, dear, your own fireside. You are my bride! No bride was ever so welcome as you. Poor hands so cold. (*Takes her hands in his, rubs them; as he does so they both at one moment see her wedding-ring.* DULCIE *withdraws her hand in shame. They look at each other horrified. A pause.*) Give me your hand.

> (*She holds it out. He takes off the ring, goes*

to window, draws aside the curtains, opens window, throws away the ring, comes back to her. The dawn outside begins and gradually rises into a full sunrise during progress of Act.)

DUL. (*as he returns to her*). Oh, you'll be very kind to me?

DAVID. I have no life, no ambition away from you. The world has gone from me. This journey to Africa—it was the object of my life—it's less than nothing to me now. I've thrown it away, I've forgotten it, because you asked me.

DUL. Ah no, you mustn't do that. Oh, I'm selfish to take you from your comrades, from your work. You must go and make this great discovery.

DAVID. I've made the one great discovery there was to make. It's the cunningest of them all. We astronomers have been puzzling all our lives to find out what gravitation is. I've found it out. Gravitation is love. It's love that holds together all this universe. It's love that drives every little atom in space to rush to every other little atom. There's love at the centre of the system. There's love at the centre of all things. No astronomer ever made a discovery equal to that! Dulcie, look at me! What ails you? What are you thinking of?

DUL. Nell and Rosy. They'll be here soon.

DAVID. Yes. They can't be long. Don't think of them. Think only of ourselves.

DUL. Why wouldn't you come with me to Beaulieu and bring them up here?

DAVID. I was afraid your sister would take you from me. I wanted to have you all to myself. When she comes here I wanted her to find you already in your home.

DUL. It's so strange.

DAVID. What is strange?

DUL. To be here with you—alone.

DAVID. It's not strange to me. You've been here so often already. In my loneliness I've pictured you here hundreds of times. I at my work in there, you in this chair by the fire, Rosy playing about the floor.

DUL. (*suddenly gets up and goes from him*). Rosy!

DAVID (*following her*). She is my child now, as you are my wife. Dulcie, say you know we have done right.

DUL. (*distracted*). Right! Yes—yes—I suppose so! What else could we do? What else could I do!

DAVID. Say you know we have done *right*.

DUL. Yes—yes—I can't think now. (*Suddenly throwing her arms round him.*) I only know I love you.

DAVID (*clasping her madly*). Dulcie, this is your home, this is our wedding-day. My bride!

DUL. (*tearing herself from him*). No, no—not now—not yet! My promise to Nell—I promised her I would take no step till I had seen her.

DAVID (*pursuing her, fiercely clasping her*). You've taken the step. You're mine——

DUL. No, no. (*Repulsing him again.*) Let me think. Wait till Nell comes. Ah, don't think I don't love you. There's nothing I wouldn't do or suffer for you. There's not a thought in my heart that isn't yours. Say you know it! Say you know it!

DAVID. I know it. What then? Tell me what's in your heart.

DUL. I can't. Can't you guess?

DAVID. Guess—what?

DUL. Oh, it was horrible with him. There was no home, no family, no love. It seemed like a blasphemy of home to live with him. But this—I can't tell you how I feel—I don't think any man can understand it. It's only a woman, and not all women —not many women perhaps—but I feel it. I can't get rid of it. To live with you seems more horrible than the other. I cannot! I cannot! I cannot!

DAVID (*very calmly, very sweetly, very soothingly*). Dearest, you mustn't talk like this. Heaven bear me witness you will come to me as pure as if I took you from your mother's side, as pure as if you had never known any kiss but your sister's.

(*Attempting to embrace her.*)

DUL. Ah! (*Shrinking from him.*) Don't I tell you, a man can't understand my feelings.

(*Looks at him half-loving, half-horrified; stands looking at him. A little pause.*)

DAVID (*same soft, tender tone, very persuasive, very*

low, very sweet). Dulcie, in a very little while you will grow to think of me as if I were your very husband—as I shall be; and with you, and your sister, and Eddie, and Rosy, we shall make one happy, one united family.   (*Approaching her.*)

DUL. Ah! that's it. I feel——

DAVID (*clasping her again*). What?

DUL. We can't be a family that way. There's only one way of being a family.

DAVID. And that?

DUL. By the marriage and love of husband and wife.

DAVID. It is marriage I offer you. Dulcie, you must see there's no future for you away from me. Say you'll give yourself to me willingly. (*Pause.*) I will not take you else. Give yourself to me!

DUL. (*after a pause*). I am yours.

DAVID. No. *Give* yourself to me—wholly, freely, willingly.

DUL. Oh! don't you see? I would give you myself—a thousand selves if I could. What is there in me that is worth giving, or worth your taking now?

DAVID. Everything, everything. Give yourself to me!

DUL. If I give you myself I give you the last four years with me. They are part of me. I shall only feel that I can never get rid of them. I cannot get rid of them! Every time you kiss me I shall see

him beside us! I cannot! I cannot! I cannot!
I cannot! (*Pause.* EDDIE *looks in at window.*)

EDDIE. Ho, ho, Davy! Ho, ho! Here we are!

DUL. (*goes to window, goes up to him*). My sister
and Rosy, are they with you?

EDDIE (*pointing down below*). Quite safe. Here
they are. Look alive, Davy! We've no time to
waste. I shall be ready in a twinkling. I'm half a
fool and half a wise man just now. In two minutes
I shall be in my right senses—or in as many as I've
got—and then—— (*Passes by, and off.*)

DAVID (*to* DULCIE). Dulcie, your sister is here.
Tell her that henceforth you are my wife.

DUL. I am your slave, your dog, your anything!
Take me if you will—take me! But kill me after.
If you don't, I shall kill myself.

(HELEN *enters at door, stands for a moment looking at one and then at the other.*)

HELEN. Dulcie. (DULCIE *goes to her.*)

DUL. Rosy—where is she?

HELEN (*pointing off*). She's there. (DULCIE *is
going.* HELEN *stops her.*) Let me look at you.
(DULCIE *looks frankly at her.* HELEN *smiles, kisses
her.*) Go to your baby. (*Exit* DULCIE. HELEN
shuts the door after DULCIE.) You've taken her from
him? (DAVID *nods.*)

HELEN. For good and all?

DAVID. For good and all.

HELEN. Why have you brought her here?

DAVID.   To make her my wife.

HELEN.   Your wife? That is impossible unless——

DAVID.   Unless?

HELEN.   Unless her husband divorces her and takes her child from her.

DAVID.   I've won her from him, her and the child. Don't come between us. Give them to me!

(*Going towards the door where* DULCIE *has gone off.*)

HELEN (*stops him*).   She is not mine to give. She is not yours to take. Your brother tells me you're going on this expedition to Africa this morning.

DAVID.   I'm not going.

HELEN.   Not going? But you have looked forward to it all your life!

DAVID.   I've wasted all my life in such dreams and shadows as work and duty. What has it availed me? Now I see one chance of happiness before me, don't take it from me! Give them to me! (*She stops him.*)   I will have them!

EDDIE *enters dressed ready to start.*

EDDIE.   Davy, old boy, look alive! The men have got everything on the mules. We've not a moment to waste.

DAVID.   I'm not going.

EDDIE.   Not going? But they are all waiting for us. If we don't go, all the expeditions everywhere will be a failure. Davy, you aren't going to sell them all like a—like a—They'll call you a—well, you fill in the word.

DAVID.   I'm not going.

EDDIE.   But what excuse can we make?

DAVID.   Any excuse you like—I've changed my mind.

HELEN (*with quiet sarcasm*).   Is that a good excuse for a soldier to make just as he's ordered into battle?

DAVID.   I'm not a soldier.

HELEN.   Yes, you are. We are all soldiers on this earth, bound to be loyal to every one of our comrades, bound to obey the great rules of life, whether they are easy or hard. Yes, and all the more bound when they are hard, when they may cost us our very life. You'll go—you'll go, and leave her to me and Rosy?

DAVID.   I love her! I love her!

HELEN.   Then save her for her child. Save her to be a good mother to that little helpless creature she has brought into the world, so that when her girl grows up and she has to guide her, she'll not have to say to her child, "You can give yourself to this man, and if you don't like him you can give yourself to another, and to another, and so on. It doesn't matter. It was what I did!"

DAVID (*same tone*).   I love her! I love her! I love her!   You shan't reason me out of my happiness!

HELEN (*stopping him*).   I can't reason at all. I

can only feel, and I know my instinct is right. I know the woman who gives herself to another man while her husband is alive betrays her sex, and is a bad woman.

DAVID.   I love her! I love her!

(Going towards door.)

HELEN *(stopping him)*. Then make your love the best thing in her life, and the best thing in yours. You have loved her so well. You have made so many sacrifices for her. Make this one last sacrifice. Keep her pure for her child.

(DAVID paces up and down the room in a fever of irresolution. EDDIE watches.)

EDDIE.   That's God's voice speaking to you now, Davy.

DULCIE *enters very quietly, looking off.*

DUL. *(to DAVID)*. She's asleep. Go and look at her.

(Exit DAVID. DULCIE is about to follow. HELEN stops her.)

HELEN.   Dulcie.

DUL.   What?

HELEN.   He's given his word to his comrades. Don't make him play the coward.

DAVID *re-enters, much calmer.*

DAVID.   Miss Larondie, I'll write to you from

Marseilles. I have left everything in order
If by any chance I should not return——

DUL. Ah! (*Goes to him.*)

DAVID. Take care of her while I'm away.

DUL. But if you do not return?

DAVID (*very calm, very bitter, very tender
little smile*). Then——we shall have played (
well in this little puppet-show, shall we not i
cry, my dear, why should you? If I were
you would tell me to go. We shall not b
from each other long. Don't cry, dear.
duty to go, Dulcie. Be brave. Tell me to ;

DUL. (*bows her head*). Go. Go.

DAVID (*going from her some steps*). I'vt
this great game of love like a fool, as me
say. Perhaps I've played the great game of
a fool, too. If we are sacrificing ourselv
shadow we are only doing what earth's best (
have done before us. If duty is reality,
done right. Right——wrong——duty——they ma
shadows, but my love for you is real. (D
sobbing, he comes to her.) Hush! Hush, dei
shall never know satiety. Our love will nev
stale and commonplace, will it? Dulcie, we
thrown away the husks. We've kept the i
part of our love——if there is an immortal part.
this is my mother's wedding ring. (*Taking
thin gold ring from his little finger.*) She ga
me as she was dying. It has never left m

since. I give it you in exchange for the one I took from you. Give me your hand. (DULCIE *gives it.*) With this ring I thee wed. As she that bore me was pure, so I leave you pure, dear. Kiss me once—I've held you sacred! (*She kisses him.*) Good-bye. No, stay. (*Pours out a glass of wine, gives it to her.*) Drink with me. (*She takes the glass, drinks some of it. He takes it from her, drains it, dashes the glass on the floor, where it is shivered to atoms; he then turns very brightly and gaily to* EDDIE.) Now Eddie—our work!

EDDIE. Ready, big brother!

DAVID (*to* DULCIE). In six months from now, come to meet me, my wife, and bring our child. Or, it may be a little later—but come and meet me—my wife—a little later.

DUL. Where?

DAVID. In that little star in Andromeda. All's real there.   (*Exeunt* EDDIE *and* DAVID.)

CURTAIN.

If curtain is called up, show a picture of DAVID *outside the window, in the full morning sunlight, the mountains covered with snow behind him;* EDDIE *is beside him drawing him away.* HELEN *has brought* ROSY *to* DULCIE, *who has the child in her arms, clasping her, her face hidden.*

www.ingramcontent.com/pod-product-compliance
Lightning Source LLC
Chambersburg PA
CBHW022338020726
47500CB00004B/1176